Up and Down the Chimney

Other Work For Children by John Fuller

Herod Do Your Worst
(Nativity Opera, Novello, 1968)

Squeaking Crust
(Poems, Chatto & Windus, 1970)

The Spider Monkey Uncle King
(Opera-pantomime, Novello, 1972)

The Last Bid
(Novel, Deutsch, 1975)

The Extraordinary Wool Mill and other stories
(Short stories, Deutsch, 1980)

Come Aboard and Sail Away
(Poems, Salamander Press, 1983)

You're Having Me On!
(Poems, Laurel Books, 2014)

Up and Down the Chimney

JOHN FULLER

illustrated by Kate Houghton

Printed by imprintdigital
Upton Pyne, Exeter
www.digital.imprint.co.uk

Typesetting and cover design by The Book Typesetters
us@thebooktypesetters.com
07422 598 168
www.thebooktypesetters.com

Published by Shoestring Press
19 Devonshire Avenue, Beeston, Nottingham, NG9 1BS
(0115) 925 1827
www.shoestringpress.co.uk

First published 2021
© Copyright: John Fuller
© Cover and internal illustrations: Kate Houghton

The moral right of the author has been asserted.

ISBN 978-1-912524-96-9

For Daniel, Felix, Joe and Ben

1. Cheese and Bacon

The little mouse was born in a cottage called Gallt-y-ceiliog in the glow of winter, when live coals fell from the full stove like bursting chestnuts and left their embers in the hearth long after the room was empty. The old grandfather mice would creep out of the stone wall to warm their bottoms, and other mice would tip-toe further into the room to look for crumbs.

The little mouse's

earliest memories were of his mother returning to the nest with bits of bread, or a cornflake. He liked to eat a cornflake, because he could nibble at it all round the edges, keeping it the same shape as it got smaller and smaller. Once she brought him a pea.

"You can eat this," she said, "because although it is green it is not mouldy. You may think it is mouldy, but it isn't. Green is its real colour."

The mouse bit into the pea. "It tastes of strange far-away things," he thought to himself. "It tastes as though it has a life of its own and doesn't want to be eaten."

He preferred food that was quite dead in itself, food that had given up all struggle and was turning into something else. That cornflake, for example. It was quite different from an ear of corn, although they were originally the same thing. An ear of corn was all very well in its way, bright and yellow like a little pillow, but it was too soft. The cornflake had become something else that needed a mouse's teeth to break it up. The same was true of cheese: the harder it was, the stronger the flavour. The older it was, the harder it was. And sometimes even a little mouldy.

Oh, the mould on a morsel of cheese! Sometimes the mouse would go to sleep still a little bit hungry but dreaming of cheese. Why had his mother said that he could eat the pea because it wasn't mouldy? Mouldy was fine, he decided. He was ready for mouldy food.

When some cheese was discovered there were always great celebrations. The grandfather mice would argue about how to share it out, and the grandmother mice would toast it in the dying embers of the fire.

The mouse remembered the first time that he was allowed out of his nest as a special treat to come to the hearth to eat melted cheese and to listen to all the mice chatting.

"The cheese is tighter and sweeter at the rind," said one. "Why do They throw the rind away?"

"It's just the same with crusts," said another. "The crust is crisp and glutinous. Delicious!"

The little mouse had never heard the word *glutinous* before. He rolled it round his tongue as though it, too, was a tasty thing. "Glutinous." It sounded like glue in a tin. Perhaps when They made bread they put glue in the tin so that the outside of the loaf would be all brown and sticky. But why then throw the crusts away? They lay on the floor beneath the kitchen table with giant bite marks where the soft crumb had been, smeared with yellow butter.

"And bacon, too" said a fat mouse. "The crispy rind, with its little skirt of fat: They even cut that off!"

"Don't talk about bacon rind, brother," came the reply. "It's a long time since we've seen a nice bit of bacon."

"I know, I know. But I live in hope."

"Sing the song of the bacon rind, brother. I've finished my bit of cheese already, and I'm still hungry."

So the fat mouse sang the song of the bacon rind, and they all joined in, laughing and belching, and wiping the glistening cheese from their whiskers:

The rind of bacon is incredible
(Rumbledom, rumbledom)
Rather like a tail that's edible
(Rumbledom, rumbledom).

Whoever's it is, he must be bored
(Rumbledom, rumbledom)
To leave his tail around to be gnawed
(Rumbledom, rumbledom).

Imagine a creature that is all bacon
(Rumbledom, rumbledom):
Without his tail he must feel forsaken
(Rumbledom, rumbledom).

Rich, and fat, and drowsy with salt
(Rumbledom, rumbledom)
Counting provisions in his vault
(Rumbledom, rumbledom).

Would he gnaw it by mistake?
(Rumbledom, rumbledom)
Idly nibble it, half-awake?
(Rumbledom, rumbledom…).

This is a silly song, thought the little mouse, about someone eating his own tail, but he never heard the rest of it because he had fallen asleep himself, and his piece of cheese had dropped from his paws, half-nibbled.

His mother picked him up gently, and carried him back to their nest deep in the stone walls of the cottage, where he had a brilliant dream about a sandwich made out of two cornflakes with the golden cheese oozing from the middle. When he took a bite out of it, the side where he had bitten turned into a mouth, which slowly opened and whispered to him.

What was it saying? He put the cornflake sandwich to his ear and heard its sleepy words. It was saying: "Rumbledom… rumbledom…"

2. Bad Boy

One night the little mouse woke from his dreams to hear a scrabbling in the wall above him. A little picture of a full yellow moon shining above a harvest was knocked to one side and some dust fell on his head. He looked up and saw two filmy eyes peering at him, and heard a flutter of wings.

He had been told never to climb up there, through the cracks that led behind the chimney, and that no mice ever went there. He had asked why not, and had been told that the fire made it smoky and uncomfortable.

So who was this coming *down* from having been up there? He looked like a mouse, but he was very ugly, and he had wings.

Perhaps this was one of his dreams. He pinched himself to see if he would wake up, but decided that he was awake already.

"Hallo, you," said the mouse with wings, hanging from the crack with his claws. "What are you called?"

The mouse was so young that he wasn't sure what this meant.

"What do they call you, silly?" repeated the creature.

The mouse could only think that when sometimes he wandered away from his mother when she had told him not to, she would call out: "Do come back, sweetheart!" Or when he took more cornflakes than he knew he could eat: "That's enough, sweetheart!"

"My mummy calls me sweetheart," he said.

The strange creature with wings laughed and wheezed.

"Sweetheart!" he said. "That's not a name. Anyone can be called sweetheart."

"What are *you* called, then?" asked the mouse.

"I'm called Bad Boy," said the creature. "I do what I want to do and don't listen to anybody. I'm not supposed to come down here. That's why I've come."

"Well, I'm not supposed to go up there, and I

don't," said the mouse.

"There we are," said Bad Boy. "We're quite different, you and I."

"We're different anyway," said the mouse. "I've never seen a mouse with wings before."

"I'm not a mouse," said Bad Boy. "I'm a bat. And I've never seen a bat without wings before."

"Well," said the mouse, "for that matter I'm not a bat either. So there!"

"Aren't you frightened of me?" asked Bad Boy.

The mouse considered the question, and decided that he wasn't at all frightened. But because Bad Boy was hanging there upside-down, he couldn't quite make out the expression on his face. Was he smiling? Or was he trying to look terrifying? The mouse leaned back and turned his head so that he could see Bad Boy's face the right way round, but by the time he had done so his visitor had scrabbled his way back through the crack in the wall.

At breakfast the mouse asked his mother if his name was sweetheart.

"No, dear," said his mother. "I call you sweetheart, but your name is Red."

"But I'm not red, am I, mummy?" asked Red. He looked at his arms, and his legs, and his tail, which were all grey.

"No," said his mother. "You are Red because Red is short for Meredith. Your full name is Meredith Munchcorn, and one day you will get to know all about your family."

Red told his mother about his night visitor, and how he hadn't been frightened.

"What is Bad Boy short for, mummy?" he asked.

His mother thought for a while, and said:

"It sounds as though it's short for trouble."

3. Fear

In the spring there was a conference of the senior mice. For safety they gathered together in the bible box under the window, amongst the dice and counters of old games whose boards they had once chewed to make their nests. They knew that it was the season when They returned to the cottage, accompanied by Their blue god, the terrible K. Who were They? The mice were very uncertain about these tall remote beings who came and went so suddenly. Who were They and what right did They have to be at Gallt-y-ceiliog? For ages and ages the cottage would be empty and the mice could live just as they wanted to. But at any time They might reappear, and when They did they would at first open the caged door of K's shrine and the slow four-footed god would stalk out and sniff the air suspiciously. K was the natural enemy of the mice, with sharp teeth and claws, but she moved slowly and could often be outwitted. She was old and losing her sense of smell. Still, the mice had to be on their guard.

Red was very curious to know all about this, and when no one was watching crept out of his bed to go and listen. He put his ear to a crack in the box and heard voices:

"There are many dangers in our life," said the gruff voice that was Samuel Crackling. "The world is full of creatures ready to attack us."

"Yes indeed, brother," said the quavery voice of Hugh Piecrust. "And the worst of it is that we are peace-loving and have no wish to eat others."

There was a murmur of agreement.

"Quite so."

"We keep to ourselves."

"We are happy with left-overs."

"What have we done to deserve this?"

"Quiet!" said Samuel Crackling, raising a paw. "This is all well-known. But we have ways of dealing with it. Take the matter of the terrible K. If we don't want to end up hanging from her jaws like a ripe berry on a bramble, we know that we have to obey some simple rules, don't we?"

"Yes, brother," said the other mice.

"When she is in the cottage, we do not leave the chimney wall," continued Samuel Crackling. "If she is asleep on her chair, however, we may do so, but only at our own risk and peril. To make the journey to the kitchen is possible, particularly if we are short of food. But there must be a chain of the bravest of us keeping guard. Even at night, when the terrible K has gone out hunting, we must keep guard."

"Why does she go out to hunt?" asked one of the younger mice.

"She goes out to hunt *us*!" said Samuel Crackling. "She thinks she will find us outside!"

'And sometimes she does," said Hugh Piecrust, gloomily.

"But only if we have disobeyed the greatest rule of all – not to go outside at night."

"That is so."

When Red heard this he let out a little cry of alarm. The elder mice heard him and hauled him inside the bible box.

"You shouldn't be here, young pipsqueak," said Samuel Crackling. "But since you've been eavesdropping, mind you take note of what we've been saying."

And while they were about it, the senior mice

reminded him of all the rules and the reasons for them. The mice knew that they must not go out at night for fear of the great white O, a cruel flying god, a god of absolute awfulness who lived in Skull Wood. O slept during the day and only came out at night, and he crunched up little mice like cornflakes. But O kept to his own rules, and the mice always knew where he was. During the day he was asleep, and at night his flying shadow swept the moonlit slopes of the fields as he looked for his prey. He was a god who belonged to no one. He was his own god.

"So," said Samuel Crackling, "let us agree to observe the rules, which are for our own good. And let us end this meeting by singing the song of fear, to remind us of those rules. And then you go off to bed, young fellow"

The mice all clasped their paws together, and sang the Song of Fear:

In the tunnel of the grasses
When the enormous shadow passes,
Fear is what you thought you heard:
Pad of beast and wing of bird.
Fear is frozen in your track,
Lonely when the night is black.
Fear has left your breath behind.
Heart is thudding in your mind.
O and K, and K and O!
There is one thing that they know!
K and O, and O and K!
Their burning eyes seek out their prey!
Remember when you go outside
There may not be a place to hide.
But fear is good, and fear is fine,
That icy shiver down your spine
Which tells you that you must be wary,
Careful when the night is scary.
However carelessly you roam,
Fear will get you safely home.

Red's mother made him learn this song, and he
murmured it over and over every night before

going to sleep. But he didn't yet know what fear was. Bad Boy the bat had expected him to be frightened, and he hadn't been frightened at all. Perhaps he would be frightened when he was allowed to go outside the cottage, and after all, if fear was a good thing as the song said, perhaps he should start going outside anyway, to have some adventures?

There was one part of the song that he did not understand. "O and K, and K and O! There is one thing that they know!" What was the one thing that they knew? It must be a frightful thing to know. Red thought that he didn't want to know this thing himself, so he didn't ask his mother what it was. But whenever he sang the song it was this part that made him most afraid.

4. Ancestors

It is quite usual for a young mouse to want to have adventures, and the reason for them is to find out things. But before he could have proper adventures, Red Munchcorn needed to know who he was.

His mother told him that his grandmother's grandmother had lived in a very smart set of floor-boards in Shepherd's Bush in London, where she was taken up by one of Them who lived there and who played the violin. The two of them had quite a close relationship, in fact, and his grandmother's grandmother even had a little mouse-sized violin made for her, which she learned to play. She had only arrived in Gallt-y-ceiliog by accident, due to this close relationship with one of Them, through hiding away in a suitcase.

"I thought They took no notice of us at all," said Red.

"No," said his mother, "that's not true. They would like to think that we are not here, or that we would be frightened by K and run away, but They do not want us to be hurt. Sometimes They are even frightened of *us*. They do not like to share

Their houses with us unless it is on Their terms. That was the case with your grandmother's grandmother. That was her shame. She was a... kept mouse."

Red didn't see why it was shameful at all, and imagined his grandmother's grandmother singing and dancing and playing her violin, living on bits of chocolate, and talking with a slight human accent.

"She arrived at Gallt-y-ceiliog in a completely exhausted state, and was kindly taken in by the Munchcorns, who have lived here since before anyone can remember. The Munchcorns are one of the oldest families here, along with the Wheatears and Piecrusts, of course. One of your Munchcorn ancestors was a famous general, General Arthur Munchcorn, who distinguished himself in the great Battle between the Frogs and the Mice."

"What's an ancestor?" asked Red.

"An ancestor is a member of your family you are too young to remember," said his mother.

Red felt very proud of belonging to this great family, but knew that he had a lot to learn. He promised himself that he would pay greater attention to his grandfather's stories.

And no amount of stories about these strange members of his family quite told him who *he* was.

"I suppose I'm not really anybody at all, yet," he thought sadly. "I shall have to do something first, so that everybody will know who I am, and can tell stories about me."

When Bad Boy next came scrabbling down the wall, Red told him about General Arthur Munchcorn.

"He's one of my famous ancestors," he said. "And I want to be famous one day."

"I can't be bothered with ancestors," said Bad

Boy. "But when I'm old enough I want to go out screeching with the boys. You could come too, except that you can't fly."

Bad Boy sniggered, and looked around at Red's things.

"What's this?" he asked, picking up a dry thistle-head.

"That's my hair-brush," said Red.

Bad Boy roared with laughter.

"You don't have any hair," he said.

"It's a fur-brush," protested Red. "And a whisker-comb. Mummy says I've got to look neat and tidy."

"Does she, then?" replied Bad Boy. "My, my. Oops, it seems to have broken."

"You broke it," said Red indignantly.

"Not me, mate," said Bad Boy. "It must have been broken already. You'll have to go around with unbrushed fur and tangled whiskers now.

Not like General Lord What's-it La-di-dah Munchcorn, eh?"

And Bad Boy let out a great fart, and disappeared up his crack in the wall.

It was then that Red decided that he wouldn't stay inside for another minute. "They" had not yet returned to the cottage, and so K was not at the moment a danger; and because it was daytime, he knew that the great O would be asleep in his tree. He had no idea what other dangers might be waiting for him outside, but he didn't wait to hear about them. He was off!

If Bad Boy was free to go where he liked, why shouldn't he?

5. The Battle of the Frogs and Mice

I t was that yellow time of spring, when all the dead brown of winter was struggling to become green again. And everywhere amongst the green was the bright yellow of the first spring flowers: daffodils, gorse and primroses.

Red was amazed at the colour, fresh and pure as the unbroken blue of the sky, but somehow its opposite. He stood at the edge of the stream with his eyes shut in pleasure, sniffing in deeply the delicious coconut smell of the gorse that grew on its banks.

"Exquise, n'est-ce pas?" said a voice at his ear. "Wonderful, isn't it?"

Red turned to see who had spoken. It was a frog standing there, still a little damp from a recent swim, and dripping occasionally from the knees.

"Allow me to introduce myself, my young friend," said the frog. "I am Gustave, Duc d'Elbeuf."

"Very pleased to meet you," said Red, just as his mother had taught him to say. "I am Meredith Munchcorn (Red for short) and I live in Gallt-y-ceiliog over there."

"But of course," said Gustave. "All this is Gallt-y-ceiliog. Up to the stream, anyway, and down into the wood. Beyond is Hendre Fawr, and beyond that…who knows?"

"Are you really a Duke?"

"Bien sûr," said Gustave. "Of course. We frogs are all aristocrats. We left our own country at the Revolution, and came over here. It was a much quieter place to be."

"What is a Revolution?"

"Oh, my dear young friend," said Gustave. "I don't think that you need to trouble your head about such things. It was a time of great danger, when everything turned upside down."

Red could only think of the upside-down life of Bad Boy. Was Bad Boy such a danger? He told Gustave about Bad Boy.

"Ah, yes," said Gustave. "Perhaps, perhaps. But I think that the bats do not want to live the right way up, like you and me. They are quite content to live hanging upside-down, in fact. Now if they *did* want to live the right way up for some reason, that might mean trouble. *Then* everything might turn upside-down. Sacre bleu!"

This didn't quite make sense to Red, but he left it at that.

"All the fresh air makes me feel quite hungry," said Gustave. "It's all this green, too, reminding me of delicious things."

Red wasn't too sure about that.

"Why?" he asked. "Do you eat green things?"

"Of course."

Red's face fell.

"Do you eat peas?" he asked.

"Ah, peas!" beamed the frog. "If only I could get them. Fresh young peas in the pod, lettuce with the dew still twinkling on it, peppery watercresses, all that sort of thing! I say, young friend, are you hungry? Would you like to come home for a bite to eat?"

Red didn't think that he wanted to eat any of

the things that Gustave had just talked about. He realised that the food he liked to eat wasn't at all green, but yellow, the colour of cheese and bacon fat, and cornflakes, too, for that matter. And he said so to Gustave. But he *was* a bit peckish, and thought it would be rude to say no.

"All right," he said.

So Gustave led the way to his house under a granite boulder that bordered the stream. Red was afraid of getting his feet wet, but once he had crossed the muddy doorstep, wiping his paws on the scraper, everything was as snug and tidy as in his own home, except for the strong smell of wild garlic.

"I know that it's spring and that the sun is shining," said Gustave, stooping over his hearth. "But there's still a nip in the air, and it would be nice to have a fire, don't you think? Particularly after a swim."

Red hadn't been swimming, and wouldn't have wanted to, but he didn't mind a fire.

Gustave started with some twists of dry grass, which soon took and smouldered. Then he carefully built up a pile of twigs.

"There we are," he said, as the fire began to crackle. "There's nothing like a little fire to make you feel at home. Now then, something to eat."

Seeing Red look a bit doubtful at this, the frog laughed.

"Don't worry," he said. "You've already made it quite clear to me that you like yellow food such as cheese, and you know that I like green food such as peas and fresh mint. Never mind. That's the way of the world. But *everyone* likes purple food."

And he brought out of his cupboard a pot of bilberry jam and some seed biscuits.

"I made this jam myself last year," he said. "You have to get up early to pick the bilberries, or else the birds will get them. So I got up early and picked lots and lots. I don't mind the birds having some, of course, and those berries that are high up on the mountain are fair picking for them, but they'd never leave any for anyone else if you let them, and what's worse…"

Here Gustave lowered his voice as he handed Red a spoon for the jam.

"… they leave their poo all over the place, on the rocks, on the paths, everywhere, and it's *purple*!"

He laughed as he settled down in front of the fire.

"You and I know better, don't we?" he said, helping himself to the jam.

Red tucked into the biscuits and jam. He liked the biscuits rather better than the jam, but didn't say so to Gustave for fear of hurting his feelings.

"You know," said Gustave, licking some jam from his lips with his very long tongue, "your sitting here with me like this in my house, having elevenses, is a very fine thing, and a very strange thing."

"Why is it strange?" asked Red.

"You don't feel frightened of me?"

"No, of course not."

"You don't want to biff me?"

"No!"

"You don't want to rally all your family, and all the other mice, and have a ding-dong battle with me and my friends?"

"No! Why should I?"

"Excellent!" said the frog. "I'm very pleased. But you know, it was not always so. No, indeed. There was once a very great battle between the frogs and the mice, a very famous battle, that was written down in a song a very long time ago, and it began exactly as we have begun our friendship now, like this, with an invitation to have a little something to eat."

Red began to feel a little uneasy.

"Don't worry, my friend," said Gustave, smiling. "All this was long ago, when battles raged at the slightest excuse. We all know how to behave ourselves now, you know."

"How did it happen?" asked Red.

"I don't have a copy of the song," said Gustave. "It would cover many leaves if I did. But I think I can tell you something of it. Have some more jam."

Red didn't want any more jam, but he did take another biscuit, and he settled down to hear the story.

"It was, perhaps, a beautiful spring day just like this one," began Gustave, Duc d'Elbeuf, "when a young mouse from a city (or was it really a cottage?) called Kalybe —"

"Excuse me," interrupted Red. "But was it the

cottage or the mouse that was called Kalybe?"

"It was the cottage," said Gustave. "But it doesn't matter what it was called."

"Perhaps it was called Gallt-y-ceiliog?" said Red.

"I don't think so," said Gustave.

"It sounds a bit like it," said Red.

"If you like," replied Gustave. "But look, if you keep on interrupting me we shall never get to the story. This young mouse was walking along the river-bank when he met a very distinguished frog."

"Was that you?" asked Red.

"No, it wasn't," said Gustave firmly. "Be quiet, and listen. This frog very kindly invited the mouse to come and have something to eat with him, just like I did, and the mouse agreed. But to get to the frog's house they had to cross the river, and the mouse couldn't swim."

Red wanted to tell Gustave that he couldn't swim either, but didn't dare to say anything until the story was finished.

"'Climb on my back', said the frog, 'and we'll swim across.' So the little mouse climbed on to the kind frog's back and they plunged into the water. All was well for a time, until they encountered a water snake slithering its way along the surface of the river. Now you never know with water snakes. They may be quite harmless, or they may be up to no good. This frog very sensibly wasn't taking any chances, so he dived down to avoid the snake, forgetting that the mouse was still clinging to his back. Oh dear. Well, of course, the mouse couldn't swim as I have already told you, and when eventually the frog got him out of the water he had… passed away."

"What do you mean?" asked Red.

"He was *fichu*, a goner, no more for this world. He'd breathed in too much water, which is no good as far as breath goes, if you know what I mean. Water in the lung? It's a big mistake for a mouse."

"Oh," said Red, who hadn't come across death before.

"When the news got back to the mouse's father, the great Filchcrumb, King of Kalybe, there was much wailing and gnashing of teeth, and Filchcrumb called an army of mice together to make war on the frogs. They made themselves spears out of thorns, and helmets out of hazelnut shells, and marched down to the river-bank, where they took the frogs by surprise. It was a bloody fight on both sides, until the sun set and they could take care of their wounded. Many valiant mice and stout-hearted frogs lay dead on the battlefield."

"More dead?" asked Red, who was beginning to be upset by this story.

"More dead, bien sûr," said Gustave. "But you

see, it was a matter of honour. King Filchcrumb felt that he had to avenge his son's death, even though it was an accident; and the frogs had to defend themselves even though it was not their fault."

"It was the water snake's fault," said Red.

"Really?" said Gustave. "You think so? The water snake was simply swimming along, minding his own business. He had harmed no one."

"Then whose fault was it?"

"My dear young friend," said Gustave. "In all the terrible things that happen in the world there is not always someone you can blame. King Filchcrumb, perhaps, for his sense of self-importance. The war was his decision."

"We don't have a king," said Red. "The grandfather mice decide things by getting together and talking about them, though some of them talk more than others."

"Yes," sighed Gustave. "I suppose that is the modern way. But it wouldn't prevent you from making war on anyone you chose, if that was what was decided. We all know that it is wrong to have battles like that, but it happens all the same."

"I've heard of that battle before," said Red. "One of my ancestors was in it – General Arthur Munchcorn."

"Was he indeed? Well, well."

It didn't sound as though Gustave believed him, but Red didn't say anything more in case he had got confused about it.

Gustave discovered that he had finished all the bilberry jam. And then he discovered that Red had finished all the biscuits.

He laughed.

"Well, that's just as it should be," he said, patting his belly. "Biscuits for you and jam for me. But it would be good to like the same things.

There's a song in that somewhere."

Red thought that he ought to go home now, as his mother might be wondering where he was.

"Yes, that's quite right," said the frog. "A young mouse ought to pay some attention to his mother's feelings. You can't always be doing just what you want to do. That's selfish. It annoys people. Rather like your friend Bad Boy."

"Is he my friend?" wondered Red. "He only ever seems to tease me."

Gustave thought for a minute, and said:

"Yes, despite all that, I think he must want to be your friend. Perhaps if you are nice to him, he will be nice too."

"I'll try," said Red.

"Go home now," said Gustave, "and come and see me soon. Come for tea. And then I can take you and introduce you to some of our neighbours. Oh, look, I can feel that song coming on:

Biscuits for you and jam for me:
We each know what we like for tea.
Maybe next time you might risk it
And spread some jam upon your biscuit?
I know you think me quite bizarre
To eat directly from the jar,
But tastes, we've found, are pretty strange
And once acquired they seldom change.
Even a simple cup of tea
Isn't everybody's cup of tea!

There, I made that up on the spot. It's called extemporising. But I must write it down before I forget it. Where is my box of leaves?"

So Meredith Munchcorn, having found a good friend in the Duc d'Elbeuf, went home to his mother.

6. Hunger

The mice thought that the presence of the terrible K had some advantages. For example, whenever They arrived, the cottage immediately became warmer. This was a blessing at Christmas, when the earth began to freeze and the wind blew through the cracks in the cottage walls. The stove sent out a steady glow, and even at night in its dying warmth the mice could explore and hope to find a pistachio left at the bottom of a bowl, or a forgotten chestnut in the ash, or even a piece of dark chocolate glistening from its crumpled foil. When They had gone, in the even colder months there was little that the mice could do but stay close together for warmth, and there was no food lying about. They found that They had left blocks of horrible firelighter in front of the cupboards, and for weeks and weeks the oily fumes made it very difficult to go foraging in the kitchen.

"We have to get used to it," said Samuel Crackling. "When K is here our lives are in greater danger, but when she is not here we are more likely to go hungry. It's a problem. Which state of things would you prefer?"

"The danger is exciting," said Jimmy Wheatear. "Just think: K is asleep on her brightly-coloured cushion, her eyes as tight shut as two walnuts. You move quickly from the hearth to the little stool and look around. Eyes still shut. You make a dash to the book case, and through the gap in the door-frame to the kitchen. You're sure to find something to eat under the table if They haven't been sweeping, which They hardly ever do. If you're feeling really cheeky you can even steal one or two pieces of the dried offering which They put down in little bowls in tribute to K, though I agree that they're not all that nice because they're oily and smell of fish. Still, it makes you feel even braver to take something of K's.

"Then you come back the way you came: under the door, over to the book case, quick, quick to the stool. And K suddenly opens one big grey eye. She's heard something. Your foot had caught a piece of paper lying on the tiles. It's only very thin, but it makes a scraping sound even if it moves only a tiny little bit. Has she seen you? Has she smelt you? Will she be bothered to do anything about it? If you keep very still, the eye will gradually close and her tail will curl again over her nose. The thrill of it! The daring!"

"We don't all find it thrilling," said Samuel Crackling. "And I must remind you of the rules. If you go into the kitchen, you must have someone keeping guard for you."

"Oh, of course, of course," replied Jimmy Wheatear, winking at the others. "I always obey the rules."

"And what is more," said Samuel Crackling, "we must learn to make our own stores of food, for the time will come again when They are not here and we shall be hard put to it to find things to eat."

"Quite right, brother," said old Jeremiah Flake. "None of you I suppose can remember the time when They did not come for nearly a year. You talked of the problem of choosing between the danger of K and going hungry. Well, I can tell you, it wasn't a question of choosing. Everything was shut up and tidied away. Utter peace and near-starvation.

"We lived for a time on a spillage of old porridge oats which we found in the dresser. It was a fine enough corner of oats in its way, but it didn't last for ever. There was nothing tasty. No bacon, no splashes of melted cheese, no lovely unwashed greasy baking pans. We could only remember these things by listening to the songs about them, and songs don't fill empty bellies.

"We came across tins with pictures on them of small beans swimming in a thick orange-brown sauce. There were tightly-sealed jars of fragrant chutney, and plastic boxes with packets inside. There were no half-open cardboard boxes of cornflakes or puffed wheat, all the easily available food that you youngsters expect.

"In our need we ate some unlikely things. Who would have thought a plate tasty? A purple plate with a border of red flowers? We found it high on the dresser after nearly a day of difficult climbing, and goodness, it smelled delicious! We hardly bothered to think why a plate should smell delicious, but dared to nibble it. It turned out to be made of old newspapers and a wheaten paste hardened like biscuit.

"Their child had made it, and it would be missed, but we did not worry about that. For a time we were no longer hungry. We shouldn't complain about the difficulty of finding food, for They now come regularly and go on being careless about what they eat. We should save something of what we find, save it for hard times."

There was a murmur of agreement.

"We should build up stores in the safest place

we can find," said Samuel Crackling, "somewhere where They will never look in their occasional attempts to clean the cottage. Many's the time when they have swept away some little hoard of crumbs before we had time to make use of them. They Themselves waste what they have already wasted. It is doubly frustrating for us."

They decided that the safest place was in a jar of gold coins hidden in the wall to the left of the fireplace.

"These things are valuable to Them beyond measure," said Jeremiah Flake. "I was told that the jar was already in the wall when They first arrived at Gallt-y-ceiliog, hidden by the previous owner. They know nothing about it. They have not looked for it, and will never find it. It stands to reason that it is the safest place for us to store food. It was well-concealed in the first place and then plastered over, so as not to be found. It is

57

quite safe, and we can get to it from inside the wall, where we live."

The plan was eagerly discussed by all the mice. When Red heard about it, he asked his grandfather what the gold coins were.

"Gold is a rare thing," said Grandfather Munchcorn. "It is a metal that does not rust like old chains on gates, but glows a beautiful yellow, like the harvest moon above a field of full wheat."

"Or like cheese?" said Red.

"Perhaps," said his grandfather.

"Or like gorse?" added Red.

"Well…not really," said his grandfather. "Its colour is its own colour, and things that are coloured like it are called gold. We shall all get a chance to see these coins before our provisions are stored there."

Red was taken, with the younger mice from other families, to look inside the jar. Their colour seemed flat compared with the evening glow of the full moon, and it was not as bright as the colour of spring flowers. But on the back of each coin was the picture of one of Them with no clothes on except for a flying cloak, sitting on the back of a horse which reared above a writhing serpent with wings and grasping a short sword with which he obviously hoped to kill the serpent. It made Red think of the old battle that his friend the frog had told him about, and about his ancestor General Arthur Munchcorn. It seemed to him that it would have been much better if the frogs and the mice had joined forces to fight against the water snakes, since it was a water snake that had caused the trouble in the first place. He thought of General Arthur Munchcorn stabbing a water snake, to the universal applause of all creatures with legs and arms. (But what would the bats have thought about it? They had legs, and *wings*. Were they really a kind of bird or insect, then?).

Into the jar, on top of the dully shining coins, were placed little tinfoil packets of cereal, bits of bacon rind, and handfuls of dry barley, which trickled down between the coins to the bottom of the jar, and would be hard to get out. But the stores mounted up, and the mice knew that in a time of great hunger they could not possibly mind heaving out the coins to get at the precious food beneath.

7. Sharing

When Red Munchcorn next visited his friend Gustave, Duc d'Elbeuf, he was, as promised, asked in for tea.

"I made this tea myself, of course," said Gustave, "from the apple-mint that grows by the stream. These are some of the seed biscuits that you liked so much the last time that you were here. And perhaps you'd like to try one of these bullace? I picked them myself last year and dried them in the mid-October sun that always surprises you when you think that the summer is over. Mind the stone."

Bullace are a kind of wild plum, and Red thought them even stranger than bilberry jam, very sharp in flavour. They made his mouth wrinkle up, and he had to gulp his hot tea to stop it turning into a grimace of disgust. He didn't want to appear rude or ungrateful.

"Very nice," he said.

"You are the perfect guest," said Gustave. "Now, I would like to read to you a little song I wrote in your honour after your first visit. I was quite inspired by meeting a new friend."

He rummaged in a rush basket in the corner and brought out a dock leaf with some writing on it. He looked at Red and gave him a little smile, then started to read:

> *Just as I am,*
> *You're what you are,*

Tight as the jam
Lives in the jar.
A spoon for you,
A spoon for me:
A friend is who
You ask to tea.

Snug as the jar
Sits on the shelf,
You're what you are
And I'm myself.
For I am me
Inside my skin
And you have fur
To be within.
Sweet as cucumber
In bread
(Perhaps it's ham
You'd like instead?),
A slice for you,
A slice for me.
A friend is who
You ask to tea.

"There!" beamed the frog. "I'm very happy to be your friend."

"Me too," said Red. "But why did you say 'cucum*ber*'? I thought it was '*cu*cumber'."

"I had hoped you wouldn't notice that," said Gustave. "But it's a very good question, and it shows that you were listening."

"And what's the answer?"

"It was a very tricky line, you know," said Gustave, "not at all easy to get right. It's the rhyme. 'Fur' and 'cucumber', you see. They're very different sorts of thing."

"Yes," said Red. "If you don't mind me saying so, your skin *does* look a bit like cucumber, knobbly and green."

"That wasn't what I meant at all," said Gustave.

"Oh please don't look sad," exclaimed Red. "It's a lovely song. And I liked the bit about 'You're what you are, and I'm myself', though when I say it, it makes me go all dizzy because the 'you' means you and the 'I' means me, whereas when *you* said it, it was the other way round, the 'you' meant me and the 'I' meant you. I don't quite understand how that happened. Did we change places? I didn't notice."

Gustave scratched his head.

"You certainly do ask awkward questions," he said. "I can sort of see what you're saying, but it makes me dizzy, too. I have no idea what the answer is."

After tea they went for a walk. Gustave wanted to pick some more dock leaves to write his songs on.

"Oh Lirrupy-loo," he said. "I do really have a song-fit coming on, and they have to be written down, you know."

But when they came to Gustave's favourite place for dock leaves, they found them all eaten away.

"It's too bad!" exclaimed. "It's that old busy-body Simon Snee. He knows I need leaves for my songs, but he has to go and eat them. Bother!"

"What will you do?" asked Red.

"Perhaps I shall declare war on him," said Gustave, carelessly. "Like King Filchcrumb. Let's go and ask Shadow what to do. She's very good at giving advice."

They crossed the stream on Gustave's raft. It was a tidy little craft made of ash twigs tied together with sheep's wool, but it bobbed about dangerously and Gustave had to keep it on course with a twig of his own, pushing against the

stones, and leaning on it to prevent the raft from drifting off course.

"I made this for you," he explained. "I normally

swim across, but I didn't think that you would care to."

Red remembered the story of young Filchcrumb's ride on the frog's back that had led to the great and terrible Battle of the Frogs and the Mice, and silently agreed.

Shadow was an old mare, who lived two fields away in Hendre Fawr. She had been a working horse before being put out to grass, and had a lot of experience of life. She was perfectly ready to give out advice, particularly if she had been brought a little present. Gustave had a radish for her.

They had to climb a gate to be high enough to talk to her. Shadow crunched up the radish gratefully, and snorted gently through her nostrils. The gale nearly blew Red and Gustave off the gate.

"I have a problem," said Gustave. "I need to

pick dock leaves from my favourite clump, and Simon Snee keeps on eating them. Shall I declare war on him? The honour of my family is at stake. The d'Elbeuf destiny is threatened. My songs will all be forgotten."

Shadow finished the radish thoughtfully.

"Are they your dock leaves?" she asked.

"Well... er, of course!" muttered Gustave. "That is to say, I've always used them before."

"Not quite the same thing," said Shadow.

"Declaring war doesn't seem the right thing at all," said Red to Gustave. "You said so yourself."

"Oh, I *know*," said Gustave. "It was just a manner of speaking."

"You seem to be sensible young mouse," said Shadow. "What would you do?"

"What about putting up a notice?" said Red. "PRIVATE KEEP OUT, that sort of thing?"

"Excellent!" exclaimed Gustave. "Why didn't

you think of that before? Let's go and do it."

But Shadow shook her mane and whinnied.

"Fatal mistake," she said. "You came to me for advice, and I shall give it. The way round this problem is…"

"Yes, yes?" said the frog and the mouse together.

"… to share!"

They looked disappointed.

"There's enough of everything around here for everybody, if only they had a little common friendliness," said Shadow. "I think that you know that very well, really. If you stopped to think."

"You mean 'A spoon for you, a spoon for me' sort of thing," said Red.

"Exactly," said Shadow.

"You remembered my song!" exclaimed Gustave. "I'm so flattered!"

So they thanked Shadow and went away to find

Simon Snee, back over the stream in the little boat and up towards the walls near the cottage where the dock leaves used to be.

Simon Snee was a very old snail, and his tracks could be seen everywhere, up and down the outside walls of the cottage, over the doorstep, and across the sheep-nibbled grass, a transparent milky trace dried to a shine, ribbons of old journeys that you could still follow, hoping that at the end you might find Simon Snee himself still slowly gliding along and squeezing out his glue. And eventually they did.

"Excuse me," said Red. "Where do you happen to be going?"

"Mind your own business," said the snail. "I don't really know myself."

"I'm sorry," said Red. "I didn't mean to be rude. It's just that my friend here would rather like you to save him some dock leaves when you're next eating them. He uses them for his songs."

"That's all right," said Simon Snee, waving the stalks that stuck out above his forehead. "As a matter of fact, I'm looking to see where I'm going *as* I'm going along. It's the best I can do."

Red realised that at the end of these stalks were eyes.

"I'd quite like to find some dock leaves actually," said Simon Snee. "I usually have some for my lunch. I think there are some more over there somewhere"

"Perhaps we can help you to find some dandelion leaves instead," said Gustave. "They're too narrow for me, and rather more delicious, I do believe, than dock leaves."

"All right!" said Simon Snee readily. "I don't mind a bit."

So they found him some dandelion leaves.

"There," said Red to Gustave. "That was easy enough, wasn't it?"

"Better than a battle, I suppose," said Gustave. "But it would have been a very uneven contest anyway."

Red felt concerned for the old half-blind snail.

"What do you keep in that curly shell you have on your back? You could keep a supply of spare dandelion leaves in it, couldn't you? And why do you leave that slimy path behind you? Isn't it dangerous? The terrible K can see where you've been, and follow you like we did."

"K isn't interested in snails, thank goodness," said Simon Snee. "And by the by, I don't *have* a shell. It's part of *me*!"

And suddenly he broke into song:

It can't be altogether right
To say I have a shell:
The shell is me as well.
It gives me height.

My route is my existence, clearly.
Deciding where to put
A body that's a foot?
No problem, really.

Look at me sailing past a hummock,
A galleon in disguise
As several pairs of eyes
Upon a stomach!

The silver stitches on the lawn
Are to repair the light
That leaked away all night
Into the dawn.

"That's a rather self-important view of things," thought Red, but he didn't like to say anything. He had never considered before what happened to the light at night-time. If it leaked away, where did it leak away *to*?

After a time they managed to find a few dock leaves for Gustave, and went their separate ways home.

8. A Narrow Escape

Red had no need to wonder what the bats thought of the serpents with wings on the gold coins in the food jar, because unknown to any of the mice, Bad Boy and his friends Stinker and Squirter McFruit had been watching from above through a crack in the wall.

"Oh my," said Stinker. "Oh my, oh my! Look at what those poncy mice are up to now!"

"I don't believe it," said Squirter. "Look at all those dinky little parcels! Are they playing at shop or what?"

"They think they own everything," said Stinker.

"Just because they've taken over downstairs, next to all those rich pickings in the kitchen."

"Yeah," agreed Squirter. "And my dad says that we were here first. The mice only came in from the fields during that great flood, when all their nests were washed away."

"That's what comes of living on the ground," said Stinker. "Stupid way to live in the first place. Come on, let's raid that food store right now!"

"Steady, boys," said Bad Boy. "Isn't that going a bit too far? You don't even like the food the mice eat, so why steal it?"

He had seen Red Munchcorn with the other young mice being taken proudly to look at the jar, and felt guilty at the thought of spoiling something that his new friend had taken such a pleasure in.

"Yes," said Stinker. "It's yucky food. All the more reason to break up the parcels and spit on the food and then throw it away outside."

"Wait till they've all gone," said Squirter. "And then we'll go down and take what we want."

And the McFruit brothers sniggered together and rubbed their claws to think of how they were going to spoil the mice's secret larder. But Bad Boy, although he *was* in general a bad boy, didn't feel like having anything to do with it. He made an excuse and left. It was the McFruit boys who did the dirty work, and who also took three of the gold coins, one each for themselves and one for Bad Boy, just to make him feel bad about not joining in.

Later, they all went out on the rampage, skidding round the roof and dive-bombing innocent moths who were out for an evening flutter. Bad Boy was particularly noisy, to make up for not having stolen the mice's food. He thought of himself as the leader of the bat gang, and didn't want to lose face among his friends.

So he shouted and screeched even more than usual and did several 90-degree turns around the chimney one after the other, till the other bats muttered among themselves in admiration: "What a tearaway!… He does what he wants to do, does Bad Boy… if there's something he doesn't feel like doing, he won't do it… he's the fastest… he's the wildest… he's a law to himself… he's just – Bad Boy!"

And Bad Boy basked in their praises, and grew wilder and wilder, and finally said:

"Let's go and terrorize Skull Wood!"

After a moment's hesitation, the other bats said:

"Skull Wood! Skull Wood!"

"Yeah, why not?"

"Creepy, eh?"

"It's got to be Skull Wood."

Now it was one thing for this gang of bats to

roar around the roof of Gallt-y-ceiliog, making a hell of a noise, catching insects and lurching into everything and everybody. It was no distance from where they lived, and it took no courage on their part.

But Skull Wood was a different matter. They had to fly a hundred yards up the drive and cross the road by the elder tree, and there was the big dark wood of fir trees. It was damp and quiet and smelled of toadstools and rotted fir cones, and here and there between the trunks of the standing trees were the grinning skulls of long-dead sheep that gave the wood its name.

There were other creatures in the wood, dark shapes that sometimes moved quickly from cover to cover. And there was a terrible sound that had once or twice come from the deepest part, a strangled hoarse cry that sounded like despair. No one knew what made such a cry. No one had ever seen it, and no one wanted to see it.

And as if this was not enough to keep even the rascally bats away from Skull Wood, it was the very place where the great O lived. In the heart of the wood was the tallest tree, with the thickest trunk, and the stiffest branches. Its very top, swaying slightly in the night breeze, seemed almost to touch the moon. Here it was that O had chosen to build his temple, a densely woven nest of twigs and leaves, whose floor was littered with the bones of small furry animals who had been unable to escape from him. He had swooped down on them in the night, softly, like a great white bedspread settling down to cover them, and tuck them up, and send them to sleep.

The shadow of that whiteness enveloped them like a dream. Their little feet stumbled. Their bodies froze in fear.

The mice of course had a song to keep their

courage up: "Fear is good, and fear is fine." But what was it good *for*? It might warn you not to go into Skull Wood in the first place. It might make you wary and watchful wherever you were at night. But once the shadow had caught up with you, what use was fear?

The gang of bats whooped into Skull Wood as

though they had no enemy in the world. They knew about the terrible O. They knew what could happen to them. But they didn't think much of it because they thought they were quick and clever. And most of them were. They could rush about in the darkness without bumping into things, because they just knew by instinct where everything was. And they didn't know the Song of Fear to remind them of the danger. Bad Boy, and Stinker and Squirter McFruit, Rollo Leatherjacket, Pete Oakbeam and little Pat Flittermouse, Bad Boy's younger brother, all entered the wood one after the other with cries of joy, as though they'd been invited to a party.

"*My* party," smiled the terrible O, when he heard the racket from his twiggy temple in the heart of the wood. And he opened one round yellow eye to see what he could see.

And he saw the gang of bats making their way

in the space between the trees above the grassy track that led through the wood to the Big Stone at the entrance to the upper Hendre Fawr field. They skittered and squawked, and frightened the ladybirds who were trying to sleep in the armpits of the trees. A family of rabbits heard them from the snugness of their burrows, and shuddered to think what might become of them.

"*We* daren't go out at night making all that noise," they said. "It's just asking for trouble."

O watched them from his hiding-place as they went past. Bad Boy was cheerfully in front, Rollo Leatherjacket was trying to overtake Stinker and Squirter McFruit, but was being shouldered out of the way, Pete Oakbeam was just behind, shouting louder than any of them, but little Pat Flittermouse was a long way back. It was only the second time he'd been out with the boys, and he was finding it very hard to keep up.

"They'll be back soon," thought O comfortably. "There's nowhere in particular for them to go, and they'll have to get back to Gallt-y-ceiliog in the end. That little plump one looks tired already. Poor little chap keeps falling behind. He'll make a juicy little snack, and the rest of them won't even notice."

And for a moment he closed his eyes contentedly, waiting for the sound of their return. He waited and waited, half-dozing. He had already eaten plentifully that night, and even had slight indigestion, but he was ready to catch one of those foolish bats when they flew by, and save him for his breakfast.

He suddenly realised that the whooping and twittering of the bats, instead of getting louder again as they returned, was getting steadily fainter and moving away down out of the wood some distance away from him. They were not returning by the grassy track, but flying right through the wood and circling round over the fields. They'd never done that before.

Curses!

O grandly rose from his temple of twigs, and flew high up above Skull Wood to see where they were. They were way down above the mushroom fields, almost at Shadow's field, and travelling at a fair bat, laughing and shrieking as they always did. O was infuriated. He swooped down from his height to intercept them somewhere above the stream, as he reckoned. Down, down he went, tracing a curved line that would eventually join the bats' own curved path like the point of a heart.

But he was just too late. They braked by the ash tree, and made for the eaves of the cottage, Bad Boy, Stinker and Squirter McFruit, Rollo Leatherjacket and Pete Oakbeam.

"Yah boo," said Bad Boy. "Can't catch us!"

But where was his little brother, Pat? He'd been fluttering bravely all the time to keep up with the others, but he was rather slow.

The terrible O's great beak opened wide and went snap-snap!

"Help!" cried little Pat Flittermouse, as he felt the beak catch and scrape at his bottom.

"Come on, Pat," said Pete Oakbeam, who was just in front. "We're there! We're home!" And he stopped to give Pat a claw and help him to scrabble under the gutter and through a crack into the roof where they lived.

It was a hair's-breadth escape, and O stubbed his beak on the drainpipe.

"Double curses!" he said, and flew back to Skull Wood.

9. Which came First?

Shadow was not the only neighbour of Red's living on the hillside, even though she was the largest. As the spring deepened into summer, and the ash trees put on leaves, and newer flowers began to appear, pink, violet and blue, Red got to know nearly all of his neighbours.

There were the sheep, old ladies most of them, who never seemed to stop eating. They went on eating and talking to themselves even when their lambs were getting into trouble. The lambs would say:

"Mummy, what can I do?"

And their mothers would just go on eating and gossiping ("Did she really?… well, I never… and what happened then?") and the lambs would say again:

"Mummy, I'm bored. What can I *do*?"

And when they still got no reply, they would bound off to the other end of the field and try to get over the fence into the road, or get their head stuck in the wire. Red sometimes found them like that, necklaced in fencing, and they were so ashamed of themselves that they pretended to have done it deliberately, and even when the wire was painfully tight around their neck they would

continue to nibble grass or just stand there with a

silly grin on their face, and a daisy sticking out of their mouth. Red thought that it must be wonderful to like eating grass, because the whole hillside was covered with it and the sheep would never be short of it. He tried a few strands, but hated it and spat it out.

What was it that made some creatures like one sort of food, and some a quite different sort? He asked his friend the mole, and the mole didn't know.

"Have *you* ever tried grass, for instance?" asked Red.

"Grass!" exclaimed the mole. "For me it would be like climbing out of my house and eating the roof."

"I suppose it would," said Red, "since you live in the earth."

"I eat what I find there," said the mole.

"And what is that?" asked Red.

"I don't think you really want to know," replied the mole.

So Red didn't ask again. He shuddered to think what it might be. He thought that the mole must lead a very damp sort of life. Why would anyone choose to live entirely in the earth, closely surrounded by the clammy soil? It seemed equally strange to live in the air like birds and butterflies, fluttering and soaring, or hanging in the currents of the air and simply gliding effortlessly from one place to another. But at least they would stop occasionally and rest on a leaf or a branch or a stone. The mole hated poking his nose into the air, where he couldn't see what he was doing, and usually after a few minutes of conversation made some excuse to retire into his burrow.

"Got a few tunnel repairs to carry out before lunch," he would say. "Nice to see you. Byee!"

The mole was always having to clear out his soggy collapsed rooms and move on to somewhere drier that he never seemed to find.

You could trace his movements across the field by following the piles of earth that he shovelled out on to the surface every now and again. Yards and yards he travelled. No wonder he was always worrying about tunnel repairs.

"It's ridiculous, really," said Red later to his mother. "A kind of mouse living in the earth like a worm! And bats, too. A kind of mouse with wings! Imagine if the birds started to try to become moles! Suppose the poor mole woke up one morning and found a redstart or a wheatear nosing its way into his tunnel and interfering and showing off like Bad Boy!"

He even wondered if the bats were really birds trying to become mice, but he knew that the birds were on the whole fairly well behaved. His mother took the sensible view that every creature was just what it was and nothing else, and what's more it had a duty to be the best of its kind and set a good example.

But Red thought that being what you are is a strange sort of thing, and he made up a song about it.

Something is swimming in the stream:
A lamb with fins? A woolly bream?
Something is flying in the air:
A mouse with wings? A bird with hair?
Of all the creatures I could meet,
A frog is a fish with hands and feet.
Any arrangement can occur:
A mole is a worm with eyes and fur,
A snail is a worm with a foot and a house
And neither is anything like a mouse.
Various parts are found together:
The worm is a shell, the shell's a feather.
It may be so, but I refuse to
Be other than the thing I'm used to.

When he sang this song to Shadow one evening, the wise old mare nodded in agreement.

"There's a rumour that there used to be horses

with wings at one time," he said. "The idea was that if one of Them climbed on its back it might fly with them up to heaven. Needless to say, no sensible horse, even one with wings, would allow that. Just think how big-headed They would get, and They are quite big-headed enough already."

"It doesn't seem very likely to me," said Red.

"I quite agree," said Shadow. "I've never thought it a very sensible arrangement. Think how large the wings would have to be to get something as heavy as me off the ground. And what on earth would I do once I was off the ground anyway? I wouldn't be able to graze or gallop, the two things I like doing best. I'd hardly be able to think. No, you're quite right. We have to be what we are."

Then, after a moment, she reflected.

"But your little song does raise some tricky questions, all the same. Think of our very dear friend, the Duc d'Elbeuf, for example. You know that in his youth he had no hands or feet?"

Red hadn't known this.

"No," continued Shadow. "And what's more, he had a tail. Well, as you can imagine, being a creature of rank and all that, he doesn't want it to be widely known that he was once a mere… tadpole!"

"I'm sure it's nothing to be ashamed of," said Red, in defence of his friend the frog.

"Not at all," said Shadow. "It's perfectly natural. And I'm sure he was a very striking tadpole in his way. But he may have forgotten that he once was one."

"Oh," said Red. He was worried by this idea. "Perhaps I was a tadpole then, too? Because I don't remember being one either."

"No," said Shadow firmly. "Not remembering something is *not* the same as forgetting something."

"It isn't?"

"No. You can only forget something that happened. You can't forget something that didn't happen. You couldn't, for example, forget that you came to tea with me last Tuesday."

"But I did come to tea with you last Tuesday," protested Red.

"Did you?" laughed Shadow. "Oh dear, I'd forgotten. There you are, then. That proves it."

"Does it?" asked Red, puzzled.

"I don't remember you coming to tea on Wednesday, or Thursday, or Friday, either," said Shadow. "*Did* you?"

"I'm not at all sure now," said Red. "You've got me all confused."

"No need to be," replied Shadow. "It's impossible to remember things that didn't happen, that's all. But if they did happen I might still forget them. That's the point."

"What about the butterfly?" asked Red quickly,

before he got too confused.

"What *about* the butterfly?" repeated Shadow.

"Do you think she remembers being a caterpillar?"

"Perhaps not. *Such* a very great change, isn't it? It will have turned her world upside down. But then, you see, when she produces babies they will turn into caterpillars, and it will bring it all back to her. You and I, we've always been what we are. Why, when I was born I could stand on my own four legs straight away. It stood me in good stead, as you might say. I was in good standing."

Shadow wheezed with laughter.

"Butterflies and caterpillars, though," she went on. "That's a different thing altogether. Like chickens and eggs, too. You know what the egg said about the chicken, do you?"

"No," said Red. "Tell me."

"It said that the chicken was just a stage in the

life-cycle of the egg."

Shadow wheezed again, but Red didn't think she had said anything very funny. The old mare looked down gravely at the mouse, and her mane stood out in a golden blaze in the light of the setting sun.

"The greatest question in the world," he said, "which no wise man has ever managed to answer, is: 'Which came first, the chicken or the egg?' But I have another, more immediately important question to put to you, Red."

"What is it?" asked the mouse eagerly.

"Did you bring me a radish?"

10. Bad Boy's Revenge

Red's closest neighbours were, of course, the bats. He still wondered if they were trying to become birds.

When he tried to suggest this to Bad Boy, his friend burst out angrily:

"Trying to become a bird? I hate birds! Particularly that great white one that chased us out of Skull Wood."

"It was very dangerous to go there," said Red.

"We're going to go back and get our revenge," said Bad Boy. "We've got wings, too. We can chase things."

"But what would you do if you caught the great O?" said Red. "Bite his tail feathers? I don't think so. And why do you have wings anyway?"

"You do ask a lot of questions, chum," said Bad Boy.

"And I never seem to get straight answers," replied Red. "I don't believe that you're going to take your revenge on the great O."

"Oh, is that so?" said Bad Boy. "I'll do it tonight and tell you all about it tomorrow."

That night Red dreamed that he was a caterpillar. It was a horrible dream that he tried to wake up from, but couldn't. The other caterpillars were doing nothing but eating dock leaves: chomp, chomp, chomp. As they ate the leaves all the Duc d'Elbeuf's songs disappeared line by line. Red told them to stop, but they wouldn't. They laughed at him, and told him to start having flying lessons. "Your hairy friends the bats can teach you," they said. "You'd better hurry, then you won't fall over yourself all the time when you become a butterfly. Oh, these leaves are so delicious! The little songs sprinkled on them make them particularly tasty!"

Red woke up crying for his mummy, and she comforted him with a piece of cheese that she had been saving up for him.

"This tastes much nicer than dock leaves," he said.

The next day Bad Boy came down to tell him about his night's adventures. They sat together in the hearth, behind a pile of logs.

"Well, we went up to Skull Wood again, didn't we? Oh yes. And we had a fine old time, me and my pals," chattered Bad Boy, picking at his teeth with an old bristle from a hearth-brush. "See, we were caught by surprise last time. It wasn't fair. So this time we were prepared. We knew what we were doing all right. We made the first move.

Always a good thing, that. Make the first move. Get in first, and do all the surprising yourself."

"What did you do?" asked Red.

"I'll tell you," said Bad Boy. "You're not going to believe this. What we did was, we got these stones. We each took a stone with us, and flew up to the wood in formation. You know, like an arrow, with me the leader in the front and the rest of my pals in two straight lines behind. And when we got to the great O's tree we dived down from above, screaming as loudly as we could, and dropped the stones one after the other, crash, bang, wallop, on to O's head. Was he surprised? You bet he was surprised! One after the other, and they all hit their target. It was absolutely brilliant!"

Bad Boy laughed and hugged himself with glee.

But Red didn't laugh.

"I don't," he said.

"You don't what?" asked Bad Boy.

"You said I wasn't going to believe you, and I don't."

"What!" exclaimed Bad Boy. "And I thought we were pals!"

"Yes, we are," said Red. "Of course we are. Well, then, how big were these stones?"

"They were monsters," said Bad Boy. "Real killers, these stones were. Pure granite. Sharp edges."

"Were they as big as this piece of coal?" Red pointed to a half-burned cinder in the hearth.

"Much bigger," said Bad Boy.

"And how did you carry them?" asked Red. "In your paws, or on your backs?"

Bad Boy thought for a moment.

"On our backs, of course," he said. "We needed our paws free to hold our sticks."

"Sticks?" said Red. "You carried sticks as well?"

"We were prepared for everything," said Bad Boy.

"Show me how you carried the stones," said Red. "Go on. Show me with that bit of coal how you carried them and dropped them. Did you lift them off your back to drop them, or turn over in the air?"

Bad Boy grinned.

"Oh, it was really cool," he said, sauntering over to the piece of coal. "You should have been there to see it."

He bent over to lift up the coal, but strained and puffed and at last dropped it. It was too heavy.

"I see," said Red, with a smile. "That's all I needed to know."

Bad Boy looked sheepish.

"Well, it was a good idea anyway. Listen, you never want to pay much attention to what I say."

"No?" asked Red.

"No," said Bad Boy. "All of us bats are liars."

"You are?" asked Red.

"Of course," said Bad Boy. "Everything I say is a lie." He gave a little shrug to his neck, settled his wings more comfortably on his shoulders, and stared at Red, with a little smirk on his face.

Red thought about this for a moment.

"It can't be," he said. "If it *was*, then what you've just said would be a lie, too, and if it *was* a lie then it *wouldn't* be true that everything you say is a lie."

"Quite right, chum," said Bad Boy. "So what's the answer?"

"I don't know," said Red. "But I expect my friend Shadow would know. She knows everything. I think Shadow would say that you are really really afraid of the great O, and that you are also afraid to say so. And you've no need to make up stories like that to impress me."

"Would she now?" said Bad Boy. "It's all right for her, bloody great quadruped. I don't suppose there's much that *she* needs to be afraid of. Anyway, there doesn't always have to be an answer to everything."

He gave a kick at the piece of coal he hadn't been able to lift, and hurt his foot.

"There must be an answer to a question," said Red, "even if you don't know what the answer is. Like 'How high is the mountain?' or 'What is your grandfather's grandfather's grandfather's name?'"

"All right, then," said Bad Boy, rubbing his foot. "What's the answer to 'What's the answer to this question?'?"

"That's silly," said Red. "It isn't a proper question."

"Well, I don't see what else it is," said Bad Boy. "It sounded just like a question when I said it. Anyway, I know the answers to your questions. They're easy-peasy. Five hundred and sixty-four metres, and Mr. Flittermouse."

"All right, then, Mr. Know-all," said Red. "Can you answer this one? 'O and K, and K and O, there is one thing that they know.' What's the one thing that they know? Is it something that we don't know?"

"Very likely not," said Bad Boy, "if they only know one thing. I know lots of things. So I probably know the one thing that they know. Would you like to come up and see my pad?"

"I'm not supposed to go up there," said Red.

"And I'm not supposed to come down here," said Bad Boy. "We both know that. So what?"

Red was curious to see the part of the cottage that the bats lived in. Could it be very different from his own? Why shouldn't he go up there? Bad Boy was a bit rude, and he was very boastful, but he was always quite friendly.

"All right," said Red. "Lead the way." He was used to visiting by now. It seemed the polite thing to do, and no harm could come of it.

They climbed and climbed and climbed, and it

got sootier and sootier, and the way got narrower. Red thought that they must soon burst out of the top of the cottage, where they might have dizzying views of the mountainside, but it got darker and darker, and soon they were in the flat space between the boarded ceiling and the roof.

"This is where we hang out," said Bad Boy. "Top of the world, eh, Red?"

Red looked at the rows of bats hanging by their claws. They weren't doing anything in particular, except sucking their teeth or scratching their armpits. One or two of them were humming slightly. Out of tune.

Red thought it didn't seem a very private way to live.

"Doesn't your family have a nest of its own?" he asked.

"This is the way we like it up here," said Bad Boy. "But just you look at this."

He took Red across a joist into a corner which he had made his own. There was a very comfortable cushion made of old spiders' webs wrapped round and round each other, and wedged into the rafters was a large circular metal disc with a picture on it of a man on a horse threatening a writhing dragon.

"Like it?" asked Bad Boy. "It's my Olympic Medal, that is. Not many of them about. Take a good look at it if you like. You won't have seen one of those before."

But Red felt sure that he had seen one before. In fact he knew that he'd seen a lot of them before, in a jar in the wall, where the mice had hidden their precious store of food. It was one of the secret hoard of gold sovereigns, and Bad Boy must have stolen it.

(Whoops, thought Bad Boy: of course Red knows what this is. What a big mistake).

11. Belling the Cat

It was proposed at a general meeting of the mice in the bible box to try to do something about the terrible K.

"She may be old and slow," said Samuel Crackling, "and we are getting better at obeying the rules. But she can still move very quietly, and sometimes when the room seems to be empty, suddenly there she is!"

"Yes, brother," said Hugh Piecrust. "Only the other day, I was returning from the kitchen with a raisin –"

"A raisin, a raisin!" exclaimed all the other mice

in admiration.

"Yes indeed, a raisin," said Hugh Piecrust. "And there I was —"

"We hardly ever see raisins these days," said Alice Munchcorn, Red's grandmother. "I've forgotten what they taste like."

"As I was saying," said Hugh Piecrust, cross at being interrupted. "I was returning from the kitchen with a raisin. It was the middle of the night, when the terrible K should have long left through the bathroom window and gone off hunting. I was concentrating on the raisin, of course, rolling it carefully, over and over. And I thought it would be easier to roll it a slightly longer way home, around rather than across the rug, where it might have got stuck in the fibres.

"Well, I was under the stool, and very near to the log-basket, when I looked up. And there was K, looking at me with great interest, not two feet away. Of course, I froze in terror, as one does."

There was a murmur of sympathy from the mice listening to his story. "Fear is good, and fear is fine," they said to themselves. "Fear is good, and fear is fine."

"What did you do?" asked Samuel Crackling.

"I knew that K is often deliberately slow and playful," said Hugh Piecrust. "She puts out a paw to hit you gently. If you try to run away, the claws come out and you are caught. She likes to watch you at first, keeping you in your place with her paws. The teeth come later."

He shuddered just to think of it.

"Well," he continued. "I had to think fast. I had nothing to defend myself with except the raisin. I took the risk of pretending to make a dash behind the log-basket. Out came her paw, and I could see a flash of steely claw. Quick as anything, I summoned all my strength and heaved the raisin against her paw as it came at me. Miraculously, it caught on the claw just as it was about to hook me. She looked in surprise at the raisin, and tried to shake it off. She hated having the raisin fastened to her claw. It was sticky. She didn't know what it was. While she was looking at it and shaking her paw, I made my escape."

"You were lucky, brother," said Samuel Crackling. "She moves quietly, and you did not hear her. We need more warning. Now, I have an idea. Here in this box, which is full of forgotten toys and games, is an old rattle which once belonged to Their child. Look, here it is. It even has a ribbon attached."

It was a metal bell, like a half-opened hazelnut, with a ball inside that rattled when it was shaken. It was the sort of thing that you could shake in time to music, when it would add a pleasant tinkle to the tune.

"What I propose," said Samuel Crackling, "is that we should, with the help of its ribbon, attach it to the neck of the terrible K, so that whenever she comes near we will hear her. It will give us time to escape."

There was much disbelieving laughter at this proposal.

"And how will we do that without her noticing?" asked Jimmy Wheatear. "The rattle of the bell itself will give us away."

"We will silence the bell with a piece of

chewed-up paper pushed inside. Then, when the bell is in place, we will remove the paper."

"But she will see us approaching with the bell," said Hugh Piecrust.

"Not if we do it during the day, when she is asleep, and They have gone out."

"But she will feel us doing it, and wake up," said Alice Munchcorn.

"This is a difficulty, I agree," said Samuel Crackling. "In this part of our plan we must be very bold. But listen, I have noticed that when They worship her, even when she is asleep, They gently stroke the top of her head. She is so used to this, that even in the midst of her slumbers she does not bother to open her eyes or raise her head, but makes the deep rumbling sound that acknowledges her pleasure at their attentions. They in turn are pleased by the response of Their god. And since both take pleasure in it, it happens frequently, simply in the course of things. If we ourselves can manage to stroke her head and make it feel like Them stroking her, then we can slip the ribbon round her head at the same time."

"Stroke her head!" exclaimed Alice Munchcorn.

"It's a mad plan," said Jimmy Wheatear. "But if we try it, we need a second line of defence. I suggest that three or four of us stand by with darning-needles, to distract her if she wakes up."

"Excellent," exclaimed Samuel Crackling. "We will prepare everything for this afternoon."

The needles were brought out from their store of such things, which they kept for emergencies, and were polished until they gleamed. The bell was tied to the centre of its piece of red ribbon, and a piece of chewed paper (a corner of the Caernarfonshire and Denbigh Herald) was stuffed inside to make it silent.

Amazingly, all went to plan. The stroking was

achieved with a comb, which two of the strongest mice wielded, one at each end like a saw to cut down trees. K purred and purred, even in the deepest of sleeps. Samuel Crackling and Jimmy Wheatear looped the ribbon around her neck, and Alice Munchcorn was given the job of tying it on with a granny knot, which she could easily do, because she was Red's grandmother. As many as five of the younger mice (including Red, who was surprised to have been chosen, and very nervous) stood by with darning needles at the ready, like long swords, while Samuel Crackling gently removed the wad of chewed paper. And then all the mice tiptoed away.

It could not have been more of a success. The terrible K was now fitted with her own alarm system, and hadn't known a thing about it.

13. Bothersome Bats

Being given a darning needle to hold on the great occasion of the belling of the terrible K made Red very proud. He told Bad Boy all about it when they next met.

"It was sharper than anything you've ever seen," he said, "and has a slit at the other end so that you could grip it quite easily."

"And they let you have one of these?" asked Bad Boy. "I'm almost impressed. Mind you, K doesn't cut much ice with us. If she could fly, that'd be different. But we're not bothered."

Red looked at him straight in the eye.

"Bad Boy," he said. "I know you well enough by now not to believe a word you say. You'd be bothered all right."

"Maybe," said Bad Boy, uncomfortably. "Look, Red, I've been meaning to say. I hope you haven't told anyone about my medal. You know. My Olympic Medal? It wasn't me that took it."

"No?" said Red disbelievingly.

"No, honest," said Bad Boy. "And I feel bad about it."

"Well, I did tell my Mummy, because I tell her everything. I don't suppose that she'll tell anyone else, but I can't be sure."

"It doesn't look very good, does it?" said Bad Boy sadly.

"Perhaps not," said Red. He was sad, too.

It certainly didn't look very good. Things had generally gone from bad to worse in relations between the mice and the bats.

"It is quite clear," said Samuel Crackling, "that all our efforts to live at peace with those flying ruffians upstairs have utterly failed. We will now have to fight them, and I'm afraid our forces will not be enough."

He was speaking to an emergency meeting of the senior mice in the bible box, after it was discovered that the bats had found their store of wrapped food and had been stealing it.

"Do we not have real enemies enough, brother?" asked Jimmy Wheatear. "The bats are our cousins, and we inhabit the one cottage."

"Cousins?" said Samuel Crackling. "Do they look like us? They have claws, but no tail. They have fur, but also naked wings. They have snouts, but their faces are upside-down. They are both like us, and not like us. And that is why we do not like them."

"I don't *not* like them, really," said Jeremiah

Flake. Then he blushed, because everyone turned to look at him. Samuel Crackling just laughed at him pityingly.

"They have strange ideas about where to live," said Hugh Piecrust. "Instead of a nice safe wall, near to the floor, where delicious crumbs fall, they live under the roof, close to the wild wind and the rain. What on earth can they find to eat up there? Flies?"

"We now know where they get their food from," said Samuel Crackling. "They steal it! Our precious hoard, carefully collected against the lean times when food will be hard to come by, has been broken into. The packages have been opened, the tin-foil torn. Most of the food has been spoiled. Their droppings are all over it."

"Yes," said Alice Munchcorn, "and my grandson Red told my daughter that he has seen one of the gold coins in their dwelling under the roof."

"If we let them get away with this," said Samuel Crackling, "nothing of ours will ever be safe again. We will have to make war on them."

"Oh dear, will we?" sighed old Jeremiah Flake. "I wish we didn't."

The meeting ended with all the mice holding hands in a circle and singing their song about the bats:

> *Creaky things,*
> *Leathern wings*
> *Upturned snout,*
> *Inside-out:*
> *What a faceful,*
> *Quite disgraceful!*
> *Bats! Bats! Bothersome bats!*
> *All day under the slates in slats*
>
> *Scratch and scrabble,*
> *Filthy rabble,*
> *Raising hell,*

Nasty smell:
Rowdy boys
Making noise.
Bats! Bats! Bothersome bats!
All night screeching and scooping gnats.

When Red Munchcorn heard about the decision made in the bible box to make war on the bats, he was upset. He remembered his conversation with his friend Gustave, Duc d'Elbeuf, after he had heard about the Battle of the Frogs and Mice. They had both agreed that it was wrong to have battles, when there would be many dead on both sides, and when after a while no one would really remember who had won. He told Gustave about the mice's decision, and Gustave said that they should go and ask Shadow what to do about it.

They took Shadow a little present of bilberries wrapped in a dock-leaf.

"Thank you," said the old mare. "I'd have

preferred something with more crunch to it, but it's very kind of you."

Gustave explained their problem.

"And you see," he concluded, "poor Red here feels particularly bad about it because he told his mother that he had seen one of the gold coins in Bad Boy's corner of the roof. He now feels that a war with the bats will be all his fault."

 Shadow scratched her chin on the gate where Red and Gustave were perched, and they nearly fell off.

"Everyone thinks I have the answer to their problems. It's because they think that I can't possibly have problems of my own, living here alone in my big field. And because I am very large.

But I don't feel large in myself. I feel just the same as you do. I just see things at a distance."

Oh dear, thought Red. Shadow wasn't being very helpful. Perhaps she was just in a funny mood.

"However –" said Shadow.

That's better, thought Red. However is always good for something. It means there's more to be said. However holds out the promise of solutions.

"However," said Shadow, "there are one or two things to consider here. If there is a war, it doesn't mean that your telling your mother about the stealing of the gold coin is the *cause* of it. From what you have told me, it seems likely that it would have happened anyway. Things happen one after the other, but they don't necessarily happen *because* of the thing that happened first. I met an ant once who had sneezed in a thunderstorm (well, who wouldn't find themselves sneezing in a thunderstorm?) and thought that he had caused a flash of lightning. I ask you!"

She laughed to herself.

"Another thing to consider is, Who in this case has behaved badly, Red or Bad Boy? It seems clear to me that Bad Boy behaved badly in stealing the coin, but that Red simply told the truth in saying so."

"But I should have kept quiet about it," wailed Red, who was getting confused by all this talk. "Bad Boy thought he was my friend. And he says he didn't take it."

"Yet another thing to consider is, Why have the bats been taking your food? Do they do it to spite you? Do they laugh and throw it away? I suspect that they take it because they are hungry, and because they don't find enough to eat up there in the roof."

Red didn't think this was true, but kept silent.

"Hunger," said Gustave sadly. "It is the cause of revolutions. My own people have been turned out of their homes and frog-marched into slavery – all for the want of a scrap of food to bring contentment."

"You should share the food," said Shadow.

"Ah, now," said the Duc d'Elbeuf, "that is going too far, my friend. If we are to give away food to strangers we shall never have enough to treat our friends. It is one thing to share something like dock leaves, which I am proud to say I myself freely do with old Simon Snee, the snail, but food is another matter."

"It's food to Simon Snee," said Red.

"In any case," said Shadow firmly, "you should treat all strangers as your friends. I do. It's a mistake not to. Then you can't have any enemies."

And with this helpful thought she turned and ambled off down her field, snorting a little and kicking the odd thistle.

"Can this be true?" thought Red on their way home. "It wouldn't cut much ice with the terrible K." He said good-bye to Gustave and wandered back to the cottage. He sat outside on a stone in the evening sun, nibbling a piece of timothy grass.

The older mice, and the older bats too, he supposed, had very fixed ideas about everything. But nothing was cut-and-dried like that. Nobody was all good or all bad, surely? And you could get to like someone who was just a little bit bad, and understand why they were like that, too.

Red was thinking all these things, with a sigh, when he heard something that made his skin crawl with fear and his fur stand up round his neck.

It was the tinkle of a little bell. Just a quiet little metallic sound, nothing much, and not at all easy to hear above the sound of the stream and the cawing of the rooks in the distant wood. But Red had sharp ears like all mice, and the tinkle was suddenly quite clear.

And very near!

He turned round, and there was an enormous blue face with bristling whiskers and a splash of fierce eyebrow above a pair of piercing yellow eyes. It was close, and looking straight at Red. It was the face of the terrible K herself.

He couldn't believe it. How could he have been so stupid? He was out too late. He had been chatting to his friends, and wandering all over the hillside, and he hadn't seen how late it had got. The terrible K was out on her evening prowl, and had found him out alone by himself.

K raised her head as if to get a better look at him, and stared down in fascination. A delicious little mouse, plump on a stone, all ready to eat as though put out for her on a dish!

Hardly believing her luck, she put out her paw

and nudged him. Red was appalled and terrified. He knew that this was what she did, toying a little at first. He had heard all the tales of encounters with her, and knew that she liked to have the little mice in her power before the claws came out.

A fat lot of good that bell was, then! It wasn't loud enough. It had let her get too near!

Red was a quick-thinking mouse. He knew that if he tried to run away her paw would shoot out and this time her claws would be unsheathed and she would pull him back towards her. It was part of her game, part of the games that the god played with her victims.

There was only one thing for it, and that was something that only an extremely brave mouse would ever attempt.

He would have to run *towards* her, which she wouldn't expect.

Taking his life in his hands, he made his dash.

He was hoping perhaps to run underneath her, but he would still be in danger from her quick claws. Instead he leaped for her arm, and ran up it over her shoulder.

K was so surprised that even though she tried to turn her neck and snap at him as he ran across her shoulder and down her back, Red was just that little bit too quick for her, and had bolted for a crack in the cottage wall before she could whisk round to see what had happened.

Oh my! What a thing! Red had reached safety, but his heart was thumping. "Fear will get you safely home" was what the song said, but he hadn't been afraid *enough*. He had been quite careless.

And he had been very lucky.

He would tell Bad Boy all about it. But perhaps Bad Boy wouldn't believe him.

13. Friends and Enemies

The summer was passing. A few leaves were already tired of clinging to the ash trees, and gratefully let go. The fox-gloves were drying out, and the sun hid itself for longer each day behind the mountain. The god K had once again been put into her shrine, and They had driven away from the cottage, putting away all the food and shutting up the windows with metal shutters.

A bee trapped between the shutter and the window-pane grumbled all the afternoon:

"Will no one help me out of here? Just my luck to get stuck here, today of all days, when I'm due back at the hive with my load of nectar."

"You could let *us* have your nectar instead," said the mice. "It would go nicely on our cornflakes."

"And why should I do that?" asked the bee.

"Easy," said the mice. "If you give us your nectar, we'll help you to escape."

And so they took his nectar and put it in a pistachio shell, and then they got a skewer from the kitchen and used it to prise the metal netting a little wider in one corner so that the bee could get out.

While they were working, they sang the nectar song to a French tune that they had heard Them playing on their CD player:

> *Nectar!*
> *It's a very special treat.*
> *Nectar!*
> *It's the sweetest of the sweet.*
> *When it's turned to honey it is very good to eat*
> *And even on its own, it's neat, yes, yes, yes,*

> *Nectar!*
> *It's the pride of every bee.*
> *Nectar!*
> *As you surely must agree,*
> *When a flower opens up it's there for you and me,*
> *Absolutely free – nectar!*

"Absolutely free, indeed," said the bee crossly, as he took his breath and straightened his wings after his ordeal. "I spent all morning gathering that stuff. Now I'll get back to the hive with nothing to show for myself. It's daylight robbery."

"Beggars can't be choosers," said the mice.

Samuel Crackling was polishing the skewer when Red went up to him.

"This will come in nicely for our battle against the bats," he said. "Feel the tip, young Munchcorn. Pretty sharp, eh? Mind you, it will take two of us to carry it, and we'll need to do some serious drill. We shall have to be deadly accurate. It won't be like using it as a crowbar."

"No, sir," said Red. "But I wanted to ask you why we couldn't have just let the poor bee go home with his nectar. We could have helped him to escape for free."

"For free!" laughed Samuel Crackling. "What an extraordinary idea. You don't get anything for free in this world, I'm afraid, young Munchcorn. Start doing that, and everyone will take advantage of you."

And he hummed delightedly as he stroked the glistening steel of the skewer.

"But, sir –" began Red, timidly.

"But, but, but!" said Samuel Crackling. "There's always a but with you young rapscallions, isn't there?"

Red was determined to finish what he had to say, and he tried to make his "but" sound as weighty and impressive as Shadow's "however." He knew he wasn't as wise as Shadow, but he did believe that he was right.

"But, sir," he began again. "The nectar song particularly *said*, didn't it, that nectar was absolutely free. So there's *something* that's free. But the poor bee had spent a lot of time collecting it, much longer than it took us to help him to escape."

"Ah, Munchcorn, you have a lot to learn," said Samuel Crackling uncertainly. He was put out by Red talking back to him. No one ever dared to do that. He didn't quite know what to say, and he couldn't be bothered to consider the rights and wrongs of Red's argument.

"We all have our… mmm… interests to protect," he said. "Market forces, you know. We have to keep our wits about us, boy. Take these blasted bats. They'll eat us out of house and home if we let them. We must stand firm."

"Of course, sir," said Red sadly, and he left Samuel Crackling staggering about with the skewer, trying to wield it by himself and falling over with the weight.

On reflection, Samuel Crackling was impressed by Red on several counts. He had acquitted himself well in his readiness with a darning-needle on the occasion of the belling of K; he was very bright, and could think for himself; and he was a descendant of the famous General Arthur Munchcorn. This last seemed the most impressive thing to him.

"I shall give him an important position in our preparations for war against the bats," thought Samuel Crackling to himself. "Anyway, if I don't, he may make trouble. That's what comes of thinking for oneself sometimes. He should think for the good of us mice in general."

But Red continued to think for himself. He had grown used to arguing with Shadow, and always felt after visiting the old mare that the world was a better place because he understood it better.

"I've been made a junior officer in our coming war with the bats," he said to Shadow. "But to tell you the truth, I don't see why the bats have to be our enemies."

"What do you mean by an 'enemy'?" asked Shadow. "What is an enemy, anyway?"

"Well," said Red. "It's the opposite of friend, isn't it?"

"It depends what you mean by 'opposite'," said Shadow.

Red got a bit cross.

"You'll say next that it depends what I mean by 'depends'," he muttered.

"I might do," said the old mare, "but I won't, if you don't want me to. But look: *I'm* your friend. What is the opposite of me? Someone with eight legs as opposed to four? Or with two legs as opposed to four? Or with toes as opposed to hooves?"

"Not really," said Red. "I don't care how many legs you've got. I like talking to you. It's not *opposite* like that."

"There you go," said Shadow. "You've hit it on the head. You like talking to me. I expect you've talked to creatures with lots of legs?"

"Caterpillars," said Red. "Bees, and so on."

"Friendly enough?"

"So-so." Red remembered how cross the bee had been.

"You feel you can talk to them as friends?"

"Yes," said Red. But it hadn't been very friendly to take the bee's nectar.

"Therefore a friend is someone you can talk to?"

"Yes."

"Therefore an enemy is someone you can't talk to?"

"I suppose so."

"Well," said Shadow. "Personally, I think it should always be possible to talk. If you disagree about something, how do you know you disagree in the first place? There must have been some talk of some kind to begin with, that led to a disagreement."

"The terrible K doesn't talk to us," said Red. "She just tries to catch us. And eat us."

"That does sound like an enemy," said Shadow. "But don't you talk to the bats? You seem to be quite friendly with one of them. What was his name – Bad Boy? Does he try to catch you? Do any of the bats try to catch you?"

"They're stealing our food."

"Well, I do agree, that's not nice at all. But you could still talk. You could talk it over, couldn't you? Talk to Bad Boy about it. Perhaps he doesn't want to be your enemy either."

Red thought this was good advice. He decided

that he would talk about it the very next time that Bad Boy came down to see him. But Bad Boy hadn't been down to see him for quite some time, and Red thought that was perhaps because he now knew that Red had told the other mice about the gold coin, his "Olympic Medal" indeed! He still felt guilty about that, but Bad Boy should feel guilty about taking it in the first place, shouldn't he?

Red didn't quite believe that it hadn't been taken by Bad Boy but by the McFruit brothers. Bad Boy was always lying anyway. He even admitted it. And Bad Boy didn't know that Red had been telling stories about him either.

After a few days, Red decided that if Bad Boy wasn't coming down to see him, he would have to go up and see Bad Boy. He really didn't want to do that all by himself, but he was now quite sure that the only way to stop the mice and the bats fighting

each other was to talk, and no mouse that he knew
was prepared to talk to a bat.

So he climbed up the dusty cracks in the
fireplace walls, on and
on, up and up, not
stopping except to say
sorry to a cross spider
whose web he broke
on the way, until he
came to the bats' roof-
space. There they all
were, folded up and
hanging upside down,

and humming in their sleep. The biggest of them
was fat Mr. McFruit, father of Stinker and
Squirter. He had big black whiskers that twitched
in his sleep, and his humming was more tuneless
than any of them. As Red tiptoed past the rows
of bats, he thought to himself: "I don't want to

wake any of them up, but I *particularly* don't want to wake up Mr. McFruit. He looks very fierce."

He found Bad Boy dozing in the corner of his pad, next to his little brother Pat. He had one wing round him, as though to protect him from harm. He didn't look bad, at all.

"Wake up!" whispered Red, shaking him. "Don't you know that all the mice are arming themselves for a great battle against you bats? How can you sleep all the time? We've got to stop it."

"Oh, I know all that," yawned Big Boy. "I don't think there's anything that can be done about it. Mr. McFruit is drilling all the bats with sharpened curtain hooks."

"Mr. McFruit always seems to be asleep," objected Red.

"Well, he is *now*," said Bad Boy. "He's been on duty all night, taking roll-call and diving practice.

He's got a lot on his plate, has Mr. McFruit. It's no wonder he needs his kip."

"Diving practice?" asked Red.

"Yes," said Bad Boy. "You hold the curtain hook in your jaws, you see, fly up as high as you can, at least to the top of the ash tree, and then you drop like a stone. You've got to be able to aim properly. We've been practising on those little windfall plums."

"Bullace," said Red.

"Those as well," said Bad Boy. "We're getting quite good at it: whee-hee-hee-squish!"

He laughed.

"Of course," he went on. "The plums are much smaller than a mouse's head, so it's very useful practice."

He caught sight of Red glaring at him, and added hastily:

"Well, that's what Mr. McFruit says anyway."

"So you're practising dive-bombing my head, are you?" asked Red indignantly. "You're going to fly down and spear me between the ears with a sharpened curtain-hook, are you?"

"Er… well," said Bad Boy. He didn't know what to say. "It's only *practising*."

"It sounds pretty dangerous to me," said Red. "It's horrid, and I'm not sure that I believe you."

"It's no more dangerous than your darn darning needles," replied Bad Boy. "Anyway, why shouldn't we protect ourselves?"

"Mr. Crackling says that *we're* protecting ourselves against *you*," said Red, in exasperation. "It's you who've been stealing our food."

"Mr. McFruit says that we were here first," answered Bad Boy, "and that you get to find all the bits of left-over food that They bring here because the food falls downwards, and you're all close to the floor. It's not fair."

"Well, that's no reason to take the food and just spoil it. Do you expect food to fall upwards? You've been opening all the parcels, and scattering the food outside. My friend the Duc d'Elbeuf says he found bits of bacon-rind by the stream."

"Not me, mate," said Bad Boy. "I don't like bacon anyway."

They glowered at each other, but neither of them felt really guilty, Bad Boy because although he was often bad he hadn't actually taken any of the food, and Red because he'd already decided to try to stop the battle that was being planned. Little Pat looked at them timidly in turn.

"Please don't be cross with each other," he said. "You're supposed to be friends."

"Now is that so indeed, Pat," said Bad Boy. "And what would you know about it?"

But Bad Boy was pleased to think that he might be friends with someone like Red Munchcorn.

Red wasn't like his rowdy bat friends, always expecting him to take them out on some dangerous adventure. Red was respectable, and thoughtful, and truly brave. He had outwitted the terrible K by running towards her instead of away from her, and now he had come up all by himself through the sooty cracks and passages to find his friend, regardless of what might have happened to him in the roof-space occupied by his enemies. He might have been kidnapped!

Bad Boy had always been a little bit frightened himself when he went down to the mice's hearth, though of course he would never show it. He had learned to swagger about and be rude just so that he could hide his real feelings. And now part of his real feelings were of admiration of young Munchcorn, who was growing up into a very respectable mouse indeed. Why, Bad Boy had known him since he was quite little. When they had first met, Red had not even known his own name. Now he was someone who had plans, and what's more was ready to act on them. "It must be my influence," thought Bad Boy. "I've put some backbone into the young fellow. There's a little bit of bat in him somewhere."

"Red," he said. "My brother is right for once. I'm proud to know you, boyo. We're not enemies, are we? And if *we're* not, then no other bat or mouse should be."

"Thank you," said Red. "But what are we going to do about it?"

What indeed could they possibly do about it?

14. Bring out your Things

The answer to his question came sooner than he expected.

In the preparations for battle, the mice were going through all their possessions, looking for things that might be useful. Samuel Crackling came round to everyone in turn, singing his ordnance song:

> *Bring out your things,*
> *Bring out your things!*
> *What have you got?*
> *Not a lot, not a lot.*

151

Pieces of string and clothes-peg springs,
Fish bones and wishbones
And other such things.
Kirby-grips, paperclips,
Skewers and toothpicks.
What have you got?
Not a lot, not a lot.
A playing card King
Will do for a flag,
A needle's a spear
And a pin is a dagger,
Bottle-top helmets
And halves of the walnut,
Nettle- and bee-stings,
The horn of the hornet
And other such things
And other such things.
What have you got?
Not a lot, not a lot,
But BRING OUT YOUR THINGS!

Hugh Piecrust produced a metal button with
"LLANAELHAEARN" stamped around the edge. With

some cotton threaded into a loop going through two of the four central holes, it made a fine shield which he flashed about on his arm.

Jimmy Wheatear's brother had a half-full box of matches, which he and his friends had once managed to lift down from the stool that stood by the stove. They had done it for a dare, and had no idea what to do with them. In fact, they had been frightened of them. Jimmy's brother had struck one against the side of the box as he had seen Them do, and had been surprised at the great blast of flame that had flowered from the end of the stick. He had tottered about with it, holding it in both hands, but it was very heavy, and it grew hotter and hotter as the end burned. He didn't know what to do with it, so simply dropped it and stared at it as it curled to a cinder.

"Fine weapons, fine weapons!" exclaimed Samuel Crackling. "Better than muskets or blunderbusses."

Jimmy's brother was glad to hand them over, for the great burning stick had singed his whiskers and he didn't want to have anything to do with matches.

Jimmy himself had a broken elastic band which he had once used to try to make himself a hammock. It hadn't worked, and Jimmy had decided he would really need lots of them, woven together. Samuel Crackling took charge of it with enthusiasm.

"This will make a useful catapult," he said. "We might be able to use it to fire burning matches at the bats."

When he came to the Munchcorns, they were unable to find anything that could be put to military use. Grandfather Munchcorn offered the cork of an old whisky bottle which he said he liked to sniff.

"It sends me to sleep at night," he said, with a smile.

"Useless," said Samuel Crackling.

"Couldn't you use it as a drum, perhaps?" asked Grandfather Munchcorn.

"Not possibly," said Samuel Crackling. "What else have you got?

Red's mother produced a die from one of Their games. It was one of a pair of dice that They would throw on to a coloured board before they could move a little silver dog or a boot or a car around the edges of it. The mouse had been quite interested in the car, but it was too small even for them, and they hadn't been able to get into the box. But the die had rolled under the settle long ago and had been forgotten. Red's mother had used it to teach Red his numbers, since it had all the numbers from one to six on its sides and you could easily read the numbers because they were written not as numerals but as little dots like this: ⚀ ⚁ ⚂ ⚃ ⚄ ⚅. Red was fascinated by the die when he was little, turning it over and over to find the next number in the right order. At first when he had reached ⚄ he went on turning it, trying to find ⚅, but of course he never found it.

"It's a cube," said his mother. "It only has six sides."

"Well," Red had said. "You'd think it might be possible to fit in one more side somewhere."

But it wasn't.

Samuel Crackling didn't think much of the die, either. "Come on," he said impatiently. "Bring out your things!"

But there wasn't much more. Red's grandmother, Alice, produced the little violin that had been made for her own grandmother years ago in Loftus Road. No one could play it, and it needed mending anyway.

"Any good?" asked Alice.

Samuel Crackling shook his head sadly.

"Drink," he said. "Gambling. Music. In my opinion the Munchcorn family needs to brace up and pull itself together. I did have hopes of young Red Munchcorn here, but I haven't seen him at needle drill for a long time, and a little bird has told me that he's actually been seen talking to a bat. It won't do. It's disobedient, and it's dangerous. What has happened to the fine old traditions of the Munchcorns? Violins and whisky corks, indeed. General Arthur Munchcorn would turn in his grave."

Samuel Crackling shook his head and went on his way, singing his ordnance song:

> *Bring out your things,*
> *Bring out your things!*
> *Bluetack for gripping,*
> *Tweezers for nipping,*

Carpet tacks, candle-wax,
Safety pins, drawing-pins,
And other such things…

15. Mending the Violin

Red was very taken by the violin, which he had never seen before. It had been made from the very thin wood of an old matchbox, buffed up to a fine amber shine with brown shoe polish. Its scroll was carved from a cherry stone and its fret was a plastic tooth that had come from a comb. It was strung with thin fuse wire and the bristles from a broom, and its bow was made from part of a tortoise-shell hair grip, though the bow had nothing to scrape against the violin's strings.

"It needs horse hair," said Alice Munchcorn. "And look, the back of the violin is loose."

"I shall mend it," said Red. "And then I shall learn to play it."

"That's all very well," said Grandfather Munchcorn, "but who will teach you? None of us knows how to play it."

"I'll find a way," said Red.

He went to Shadow for some horse hairs.

"I think they use hairs from a horse's tail," he said. "Can you spare a few?"

"What," said Shadow, "a poor old mare like me? I don't have enough hairs left for my own use. What am I going to use to flick away the flies if I don't have a tail?"

"Oh, *please*," said Red. "Dear Shadow, dear kind old Shadow, just a few. I only need a very few."

"All right, then," said Shadow. "But my tail hairs are surely too thick for that tiny little violin. You can have one or two from my eyebrows. I don't much care for those, anyway."

Red climbed up Shadow's nose and took five white hairs from her eyebrows.

"Ouch," said Shadow. "That made my eyes water."

"Shadow," said Red. "You're a real friend. I'll bring you a peppermint –"

"Oh, thank you," said the grateful mare.

"– whenever I next find one," continued Red.

"Oh, I see," said Shadow, a little disappointed. "You mean you don't already have some at home?"

"No, I'm afraid not," said Red.

"Well, never mind," said Shadow. "I shall look forward to the day when you do. I'm always looking forward to that day. It never comes."

"I'll do my best," said Red.

After leaving Shadow, Red visited the largest spider he knew, who happened to live in the bathroom.

"I need something to stick a lot of things together," said Red.

"What sort of things?" growled the spider.

"Oh, bits of matchwood, and horse's eyebrows, that sort of thing," said Red lightly. "Can you give me some of the stuff you use to hold your web together? I know it's very strong."

"Well, you've got a cheek, I must say," said the spider.

"I know it's very strong, because everyone says that you make the strongest webs of all, stronger than any of the garden spiders."

"It's true," said the spider, who was pleased to hear this. "I am, after all, a Mouse Spider, Scotophaeus Blackwalli, and there aren't many of my kind hereabouts."

"A Mouse Spider!" exclaimed Red. "That's lucky. Perhaps we are related?"

"I don't think so," said the spider firmly. "No. I

don't really have any relations."

"Oh dear," said Red. "Aren't you lonely?"

"Have you ever seen a spider who looks lonely?" said the spider. "I am the centre of the entire universe. I love it when They've gone, and I can have the whole bath to myself."

"In that case," said Red. "You won't mind letting me have some of that gluey stuff that you spin out of your tummy, will you?"

"You're brazen, you are," said the spider. "Oh, all right then. But I can't let you have very much. You'd better bring the things you want gluing in here, and I'll do it for you."

When Red came back, the spider smiled.

"You didn't say it was a *violin*," he said.

"So you've seen one of these before?" asked Red.

"Oh well," said the spider, as he deftly applied the layers of sticky stuff from his stomach, "I wouldn't say that, exactly, but I've seen pictures of them. They're supposed to be very good at charming flies, I believe. A few bars of Brahms and the flies are absolutely transfixed. Can't move a muscle. You can do what you like with them. Wham! There, it's done."

Red took the violin back. The back of it was no longer loose, and the hairs were now firmly glued to the bow, neatly side by side.

"That's wonderful," he said. "You must have done this before."

"Never in my life," said the spider. "But it's a doddle compared to flinging gossamer across great distances and making it stick to shiny things like bath taps."

"Yes, I expect it is," said Red. "I'm ever so grateful, though. How can I thank you?"

"Well," said the spider thoughtfully. "I am feeling quite hungry at the moment. I don't suppose you can play any Brahms, can you?"

"I'm afraid not," said Red. "But I can learn to."

"You do that," said the spider, "and then come back here. A bit of Brahms would be very useful."

But who could teach Red how to play the violin? His grandparents had never learned how to, and nor of course had his mother. He asked Bad Boy if any of the bats could play. They were in Red's little room, passing the time of day.

"We're all very talented at music," said Bad Boy. "You've heard us humming, haven't you?"

Red had indeed heard the bats humming, and hadn't thought much of it, but he didn't say so.

"And I can play the drums," said Bad Boy. "Blackety-blackety-blackety-*smash*! Blackety-blackety-blackety-blackety-blackety-dunk-dunk-*smash*! Blackety-blackety-blackety—"

"Yes," said Red. "I get the idea. That's very good. You're all brilliant at humming and drumming and that sort of thing, but I need to learn how to play the violin. A bit of Brahms, possibly, if I can. Whatever that is."

"Good luck to you, mate. I can't think why you're bothered, but good luck anyway."

"I can't quite think why, either, but it seems like a good idea."

At that moment a little spillage of dust mixed with soot fell on their heads, and a fierce bewhiskered face thrust itself through a crack above them. It was Mr. McFruit!

"What's this?" he shouted. "What are you doing down here, Bad Boy, you bad boy!"

He looked around the room, half-blind with big red-rimmed eyes.

"It's you, isn't it?" Mr McFruit said to Red. "You pompous stuck-up little mouse. If I could squeeze through this crack I'd give the both of you what-for."

He grunted and pushed and wheezed, but he was too fat to get through. Nearly as fat as Samuel Crackling, thought Red. Why were these two so fat *and* warlike? They weren't particularly clever or brave. They were even a bit silly.

But Red was quite frightened of Mr McFruit. And so was Bad Boy.

16. A Bit of Brahms?

When Red drew the bow across the strings of the violin, it made a dull whispering sound, like the evening wind blowing through the fir-trees in Skull Wood. That didn't seem right at all.

He asked his grandmother about it.

"I've told you, Red," said his grandmother. "I've no idea how it works. I never saw my own grandmother playing it. My mother found it wrapped up in one of those red and white sheets that They use to blow Their noses on. I don't think she ever heard it played either."

"Somebody must know," thought Red. He knew very well who his grandmother was, but he still couldn't quite get used to the idea of his grandmother having had a grandmother of her own.

"Grandma," he said.

"Yes, Red?"

"Did your grandmother have a grandmother of her own?"

"Yes, she did."

"And did *she* have a grandmother, too?"

"Yes, of course she did."

"So where are they all?" asked Red.

"They are all dead now," said Alice Munchcorn. "They lived a long time ago."

Red thought about this, but it made him dizzy after a bit, and it was frightening to think about, too. When mice died, they disappeared. But where did they go to? He didn't want to think about it much.

He took the violin and went out on to the hillside. He thought of asking the mole if he knew anything about violins, and knocked on the freshest-looking of the molehills that peeped above the grass.

"Not at home, not at home!" said the pink snout that pushed its way through the loose earth.

"Of course you're at home," said Red. "I can see you."

"Well, *I* don't want to see anyone," said the mole. "Particularly not a mouse. Or a bat. I've heard that they're preparing for a great war against each other. It will be utter chaos. *So* irresponsible. I shan't be able to show myself above ground, so I shan't know where I am any more."

"You can't see much anyway," said Red.

"Well, I've got to get my bearings, haven't I?" said the mole. "I can't burrow directly into the mountain, can I? I've got to keep an idea of the lie of the land. And if I do come up I shall probably be run through by a mouse, or dive-bombed by a bat. You're not carrying a weapon, are you?"

"No," said Red. "Only this."

He showed the mole his violin.

"Oh my goodness!" exclaimed the mole, blinking at it in terror. "What on earth is that? Don't point it at me, don't point it at me! It might go off!"

"It won't go off," laughed Red. "It's a musical instrument."

"What's that?" said the mole. "An instrument? It's an instrument of torture! Oh please don't torture me. Go away, go away!"

And the mole burrowed quickly back into the earth. Red thought he was  being very silly, but at the same time he was worried that all the preparations for war were making everyone so frightened. It was one thing for the mice to be frightened and the bats to be frightened, because they were all angry at each other and frightened of what the other's anger might do. But now that all the animals on the hillside had heard about it, the fear was widespread. Might some of the animals take sides? Perhaps the whole mountain would become a theatre of war.

"You are looking very sad, my friend," said a voice at his ear. It was Gustave.

"Why, Gustave!" said Red. "I haven't seen you for ages. What are you doing up here so far from the stream?"

"As you can see," said Gustave, showing him a basket, "I've been blackberrying. I've picked all those growing near the stream, and I've been looking for more in the field behind Gallt-y-ceiliog. I should have known better. There aren't any. But what is the matter with you?"

"Oh, I don't know," said Red. "Everyone is quite certain that fighting is going to break out any day now, and there's no reason for it, none at all. I'd much rather we all formed a band. That's my big idea at the moment."

What a surprise! It was a surprise even to Red, because in truth he had really only thought of it at that moment. No one had bothered to ask him what the matter was. Even Shadow seemed to have forgotten all about the mice and bats arming themselves, and hadn't mentioned it again. Well, she was so big, and lived so far away, she would hardly be affected by it, would she?

"A band!" said Gustave. "What a fine idea! Now I understand why you're carrying a violin. You have become a violinist and are going to lead a hillside orchestra."

"I wish I could," said Red. "But I've tried to mend it and it doesn't work. Nobody knows how to play a violin here."

"Oh, but I do," said Gustave. "I can play very well, as a matter of fact. All the best violin music."

Red was amazed.

"But that's wonderful!" he exclaimed. "You can teach me. Do you know any Brahms?"

"Brahms?" said Gustave, pulling a face. "Certainly not. He's far too heavy and Germanic for me. I like Sarasate, and Ysaye. Ravel, perhaps. Something dashing, with a touch of the gypsy in it."

"You won't be able to play anything dashing with this," said Red sadly. "Listen, it sounds like dried leaves."

"Oh goodness me," said Gustave impatiently, taking the violin from him. "You don't play it on your knee like that. You look as though you're cutting a loaf of bread."

The frog put the violin beneath his chin and twiddled the pegs that held the strings near the scroll. He tried the bow once or twice, but the violin still seemed loose and out of tune. Nonetheless, he played a few phrases of what seemed like a jaunty tune, heard through a storm.

"Oh, aren't you clever!" said Red.

"It's the Triumphal March from Bizet's little-known opera *Les Fiançailles de Grenouille*, Frog Wedding."

"When did you learn to play?" asked Red.

"Oh, it's in the family, of course," said Gustave carelessly. "An early ancestor of mine was at the court of King Louis the Sun King and was a great friend of the composer Lully. Mind you, he lived rather humbly in a gilded fish-tank and was brought out at dessert to amuse the guests. But since he could play the music of Lully, which was unusual for a frog at that time, you can imagine the impression he made. It was so unusual that he was ennobled by the King, and created the first Duc d'Elbeuf.

"Really?" asked Red, politely.

"Oh yes," said Gustave. "It is the most distinct honour in our family. The composer Lully, as you must know, invented the cradle song, the music that sends baby frogs and mice to sleep. That's why they're called lullabies."

"Really," said Red yet again. Was Gustave going to go on talking for ever? Red wondered if he were making it all up as he went along.

"Indeed," said Gustave. "I shall play you one. Let me see, how does it go?

He tucked the violin under his chin, and drew the bow up and down the strings once again. The sound was more like the bleating of a sheep than anything else.

"Oh, damn it all!" said Gustave suddenly, stamping his foot. "That's Brahms, isn't it? Why on earth did you have to mention him? Now I'm playing his cradle song."

He tried again.

"No," said Gustave. "It's hopeless. I can't get the thing out of my head now."

He lowered the violin and looked at Red in exasperation. Then he laughed, and Red had to laugh with him, though he wasn't really sure what they were laughing about.

"You'll be able to hypnotise flies now," said Red. "The bathroom spider will be very pleased."

"I have no intention of pleasing the bathroom spider," said Gustave. "Now look: come to me tomorrow afternoon and I promise I'll have the violin in tip-top shape for you. I'll have to tighten these pegs, and we need some rosin for the bow. I think some dried resin from old fir-cones in Skull

Wood should do the trick."

"Oh, do be careful," said Red. "You have to be careful going into Skull Wood."

"I know what I'm doing," said Gustave. "Don't worry. I was going in any case, to look for mushrooms."

17. The Ultimatum

The frog's expedition was a success. The resin from the fir cones, little hard globs that rubbed to a powder, gave a fine grip to the hairs of the bow so that it made a rich vibrating sound,

and it helped to tighten the pegs, too, so that the strings could be properly tuned. When Gustave now played the Triumphal March from Bizet's *Frog Wedding*, it resounded throughout his little parlour and made the dishes dance on the dresser.

"Good, eh?" said Gustave, immensely proud of himself. "It's a well-made instrument, this one, I have to say. It even makes Brahms's cradle-song seem worth listening to. Though I still like French music much more."

He played the little lullaby with his eyes shut, swaying slightly with dreamy pleasure.

"Now you try," he said to Red. "Put your fingers on the string just here. Lift this finger. Now put it down again. Do you see the difference between the notes? Now this other finger up here. That's another note altogether! You'll soon get the hang of it."

Red was pleased with himself for being able to play three notes, and sat down rather red in the face while Gustave poured them some mint tea.

"I sound dull and flat," Red complained. "How do *you* make it sound so thrilling?"

"Ah," said Gustave. "That's a bit tricky. You have to move your finger from side to side on the string, gently and regularly, as though you were rubbing something out."

"Like this?" asked Red.

"Not quite," said Gustave. "Never mind. I'll show you later. It's called 'vibrato.' Let's have some mushrooms now. I found lots."

He put a little oiled frying pan on the stove, and popped in a handful of sliced russula with a sprinkling of garlic and pepper. Soon a heavenly smell filled his whole house.

"Isn't it simply delicious?" he said, with the plate on his knee, lifting a forkful to his mouth. "It's like the essence of the earth itself, and all the good things that come from it. I love these days of autumn. They remind you that nothing lasts for ever. I wrote a song about it."

Gustave dipped into his song basket and came up with a sycamore leaf with one of his songs written on it:

> *Like russula against the moss*
> *Or like the geese that fly across*
> *Their coloured woods with creaking wings*
> *Or like the first lit twig that sings*
> *To friends at talk before a fire*
> *With hot mint tea as flames leap higher,*
> *We are like this, a hopeful song*
> *That thrills the ear but won't last long:*
> *The pink and grey caps rot, the feather*
> *Falls, the woods are hurt by weather,*
> *The hearth grows cold and friends are parted,*
> *And we, like the tea-pot, empty-hearted.*

"I don't think that's a very hopeful song," said Red, wiping a tear from his eye. "It seems like a sad song to me."

"They're often the same sort of thing," said

Gustave. "You can look forward to something at the same time as being sorry that something else has passed. And all these things we love, they don't last long. They come and go. We have to enjoy them while we can."

"I suppose we do," said Red.

"Come," said his friend. "Let's be cheerful. Have some more of these delicious fungi."

Red took another helping. He didn't know 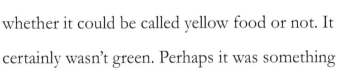 whether it could be called yellow food or not. It certainly wasn't green. Perhaps it was something in-between.

Gustave had gathered so many fungi that he ate them every day, and those that he couldn't eat he dried and strung on rushes which he hung from his ceiling: fat withered slices of Wood Blewit, shrunk cubes of Red-staining Boletus and little shrivelled twists of Amethyst Deceiver.

"You've got to know what you're picking, of course," he said. "Some of them can give you a nasty upset tummy, and they look just as beautiful as all the others, and smell just as nice. Come tomorrow and we'll eat some Parasols with butter. And we'll have another violin lesson."

Red came every day, and soon could play the violin quite well. At least, he could play Brahms's cradle-song quite well. Ysaye was beyond him, since it seemed to involve walking the fingers quickly right up to the chin and back again, while the bow bounced up and down on the strings. Even Gustave found it quite hard, since his upper lip became rigid and his eyes popped, and a frown wrinkled the marbled green skin of his forehead. And in the middle of it he would suddenly stop, lower his bow and laugh.

"I'm not quite up to this!" he would exclaim.

"Let's make a fresh pot of tea!"

Back at the cottage, the preparations for war had reached a climax. In the bats' attic the sound of humming and snoring had been replaced by hammering all night, and in the dusk, instead of their usual twittering and flittering here and there to no great purpose, the bats had started to fly swiftly and silently together in aerial formation. A line of three or four of them would soar out from the roof and suddenly swoop all together till they nearly touched the ground, then rise again, keeping in a straight line. They practised this until they could bite the heads off the dried clover. And they went on searching for curtain hooks.

The mice had collected together all the weapons they could think of, and even Samuel Crackling was pleased by their efforts. For himself, he had found a green and black toy digger, lost in cobwebs behind the bible box. He cleaned it up, and tied cotton strings to the shovel part so that when he sat on it and pulled on them, the arms would rise and the shovel's toothy jaws would open and close. It couldn't actually be made to pick anything up, but as Samuel Crackling's busy arms pulled first one string and then the other, the digger looked like a mechanical dragon ready to devour its enemies. He was delighted with it, and insisted that two or three mice should push him into battle on it. He kept falling off, of course, because he was too fat and had to perch on top of the cab instead of sitting inside it, but he thought that the digger made him look ferocious, and he oiled his whiskers until they gleamed.

This was all very well, but where would the field of battle be? And what would spark the conflict? Samuel Crackling was quite ready to order the battalions of mice into action: row upon row of needle-spearmen, platoons of mixed weapons (including a recently-found toothbrush ready to be set alight and used as a battering-ram), a team to work the catapult, and so on. He himself would ride at the head of them on his green digger, wearing a brass thimble as a helmet. But where were they to do this? They couldn't climb up the chimney in full battle array to meet the bats in their roof space. They would be exhausted, and couldn't get all their equipment up there.

"And if we prepare ourselves in the hearth, as we have been doing," said Jimmy Wheatear, "it seems very unlikely that the bats will come down to meet with us, just because we are there ready for them. It all seems a waste of time to me."

"But we must prepare ourselves," said Samuel Crackling. "It takes time to move our equipment."

"Exactly," said Hugh Piecrust. "So what if the bats attack us when we are not ready? We can't be lined up in battle array all our lives."

"We should issue a challenge," said Crackling. "Someone should go up to the bats and deliver an ultimatum."

"What's an ultimatum?" asked Jimmy Wheatear.

"I think it might be a sort of button," said Crackling uncertainly. "Anyway, they'd have to accept it, under the rules of war."

"Suppose they don't accept it?" asked Wheatear.

"Then it is war!" replied Crackling.

"Suppose they *do* accept it?"

"Then it is certainly war!"

Jimmy Wheatear and some of the other mice didn't think this sounded quite right, but there was no arguing with Samuel Crackling, especially when he was already wearing his thimble.

"Now," said their intrepid leader, "we must find someone who will deliver the ultimatum, and I think I know who it will be. A young mouse who has courage, and a sense of adventure. A spirited young fellow who has shown himself nonetheless willing to benefit from the advice of his elders and betters. A mouse who has had to struggle against the soft-centred attitudes of his family. A mouse, moreover, who knows how to find his way up the chimney. Most important, that. Who is the mouse I am referring to? It is Meredith Munchcorn!"

18. Battle Lines

It was with a heavy heart that Red started to climb the chimney, carrying the metal LLANAELHAEARN button that Hugh Piecrust had been using as a shield. No one had clearly told him what might happen to this "ultimatum" when it was presented to the leader of the bats, Mr. McFruit. Hugh Piecrust thought, sadly, that he might even spit on it.

"I shall never be able to use it again," he said.

"If it is mistreated," proclaimed Samuel Crackling, "you may take a personal revenge. We shall all bear that in mind."

Red was nervous of what he would find in the bats' attic. He was very frightened of Mr McFruit, who was already promising to give him "what-for" (whatever that was). Perhaps he would seize his button and hold him prisoner. You were allowed to take prisoners in war, though you weren't allowed to mistreat them. But he was approaching the bats as an envoy, a messenger. They would have to listen to what he was going to say, even though he didn't know himself what he was going to say.

But half-way up the chimney, Red had a shock.

There, coming down to meet him, was Bad Boy!

And just as Red was carrying his button-ultimatum (with some difficulty, as it got in his way when he was squeezing between crevices, and had to be hauled up over the stones) so Bad Boy had his own circular object which he found hard to carry.

It was his Olympic Medal, the golden guinea that had been stolen from the mice's food jar!

"What on earth are you doing?" said each of them to the other.

"I'm bringing you an ultimatum," said Red.

"Well now, that's a funny thing," said Bad Boy. "So am I."

"Do you know what it is meant to be?" asked Red.

"No idea," replied Bad Boy. "I wasn't sure whether it was a kind of threat or a sort of peace offering."

"I don't think mine is meant to be that," said Red. "Mr. Crackling would be very disappointed if the battle was called off."

"I think Mr. McFruit would be, too," said Bad Boy.

"What shall we do with these ultimatums, then?"

"I haven't a clue."

"Nor have I."

"They're all waiting for us. Mr. McFruit says that if the battle goes ahead we'll knock you all into next week, so you might as well give up."

"Mr. Crackling rather thinks the same, but seems to want to fight anyway."

"I wish they had something better to do."

"So do I."

"Perhaps this is the moment to put your plan into action?"

"Yes, I think it is."

The two friends were eagerly awaited by their respective armies, but neither of them returned the way they had come. They had a secret place in the chimney which they had found during the summer. No one else ever came there because they were all too busy being drilled for the battle, and besides, they didn't dare to follow, because secret places are extremely special, whether they belong to one person, or very rarely, two. There is a song about them:

Secret places
That no one's seen,
Hidden spaces
In between.
He's suddenly back!
Where has he been?
Up in an attic,
Down in a crack.
Know what he's at?
He's being alone.

Someone's not here.
Someone has gone.
Someone knows~
How to disappear.
And off he goes
Where you can't find him
(You mustn't mind him,
Don't mind a bit:

He's having a fit
Of being alone).

Do you suppose
He's on his own?
Or will he share?
Pretend it's a game:
Follow him there
And call his name.
If no one replies
You'll have to decide
To stay outside.
He's being alone.

But somehow Red and Bad Boy *had* found each other there, and it was a place well away from the noisy show-off McFruits and the disapproval of Samuel Crackling. It was in fact a place where they could be alone *together*. It was a place in the chimney that belonged neither to mouse nor bat. Just the place to plan something.

Back in the attic and the hearth, the waiting bats

and mice became impatient. Each side thought that the other was ignoring them, and what was worse, holding their representative hostage.

"Oh dear," said Alice Munchcorn. "Why hasn't Red returned? Perhaps the bats have tied him up to a chimney-pot and are covering him with soot. Or worse."

"Oh dear," said Mrs. Flittermouse. "Why hasn't Bad Boy come back? Perhaps the mice have tied him to the poker and are covering him with ash. Or worse."

"The bats are capable of anything," said Samuel Crackling. "We must attack at once."

"The mice just won't listen to us at all," said Mr. McFruit. "We'll have to prepare to defend ourselves."

But how could the mice climb up the chimney with all their armour and equipment? It was not only Samuel Crackling with his thimble helmet, riding on his green digger with two assistants pulling strings, but all the spears and shields and catapults and snapping scissors and matchboxes and things. The best they could do was to assemble in battle order, rank after rank, pulling ferocious faces.

But try as he might, a mouse isn't really designed to pull a ferocious face. When he frowns he simply looks pathetic, and when he bares his teeth it immediately looks like a smile. Doing both together doesn't look a bit angry. It's as though he's pleading to be given a treat. Snarl, snarl (give us a treat!). Snarl, snarl (give us a treat, do!).

So when Samuel Crackling led them all out of the cottage to parade up and down on the close-cropped grass, looking as fierce as they could, challenging the bats to come and fight them, they only succeeded in looking sly and wheedling. And when the bats came out from under the eaves, three by three, gripping their own weapons, pins and needles, lit candle-stumps, and sharpened curtain-hooks, they looked down and saw fat Samuel Crackling grimacing on his digger and they all burst out laughing.

"Look!" cried Squirter McFruit. "Old Samuel Crackling is trying to do a poo, and can't! He's all gummed up!"

"But he's got a big enough grabber ready for it!" added Stinker.

"Be quiet, you boys," said Mr. McFruit. "This is no joke."

And it wasn't. Samuel Crackling was really furious. He ordered Jimmy Wheatear and his brother to draw back the strong elastic of their catapult and to scrape the first of their matches against the side of the box (for which they needed the help of two further mice). The bats, in response, lifted their sharpened curtain-hooks and hung poised from the gutters, ready to swoop. It seemed that nothing could prevent the battle from beginning right away.

Yet just at that moment a sound was heard that stopped everyone in their tracks. It was a beautiful musical sound coming from behind the cottage, a sound that seemed designed to calm every angry nerve, a gently rocking tune, tender but firm like a hand on a cradle.

As the warlike mice looked at one another in amazement and the bats hanging from the gutters strained to catch the melody, the sound of the music got louder and louder as the pair who were performing it came round the side of the cottage, across the stones, to take up their position just between the two armies.

It was Meredith Munchcorn and Bad Boy Flittermouse, of course, on violin and drums, with extra harmonic humming from Bad Boy. Red was playing the family violin as well as he had ever played it, with no more than about one slightly wrong note in every six. Bad Boy's drums were a stroke of genius. He had made them from a pair of cracked ping-pong balls that he had found in the long barn at the side of the cottage, strung round his neck. When he patted and stroked them they made a jolly sound half-way between dripping water and the tick of a clock.

The two armies were mesmerised. The Wheatear brothers nearly burned their fingers from the match they had struck and now had to drop quickly. Three bats lost their footing and tumbled from the roof. Mice lowered their darning needles in wonder, and Samuel Crackling's thimble fell off.

19. Oh, No!

It was quite clear that the battle could not now proceed. Both sides were completely changed by the music, lulled and pacified by the tune and absorbed by the rhythm. They were almost as hypnotised as the flies were, who hung above them in a wavering cloud of rapt bliss. Besides, the musical duo had now positioned themselves on a slate by the corner of the cottage, exactly in the middle of the armies. If any weapons were now to be launched there would be a grave risk of hurting someone from your own side, and nearly all the mice and bats were relieved to realise it.

They all suddenly knew that they had no appetite for fighting at all.

"Hurrah for Red Munchcorn!" cried Alice Munchcorn proudly.

"Hurrah for Bad Boy Flittermouse!" shouted his little brother Pat.

"Hurrah for Red!" shouted all the bats.

"Hurrah for Bad Boy!" shouted all the mice.

"Down with Mr. McFruit," shouted the bats.

"Down with Mr. Crackling," shouted the mice.

Samuel Crackling attempted to make a speech.

"Fellow-mice," he said. "I have to say this. I have always acted according to my sincerely-held beliefs and in your best interests —"

"Rubbish," said Jimmy Wheatear. "You never listen to us at all. Little Red Munchcorn is twice the mouse you are."

And Jimmy blushed at his daring, looking round sheepishly at all his friends.

"Well said, Jimmy," they all said.

"Yes, well," said Jimmy. "We shall all have to learn to live together, shan't we? And if we can have concerts like this every week, I don't see why we can't."

"We'd better get inside, though," said Hugh Piecrust. "It's getting dark."

"Yes," said Alice Munchcorn. "It's the dangerous hour."

And so they would have gone back inside quite safely, except that at that very moment the slate that the musicians had been playing on began to move. It shifted about like a small earthquake, and crumbs of soil were pushed out beneath it.

It was the mole.

Deep in his damp tunnel as he burrowed his damp way from nowhere in particular to nowhere else, he had heard the music above him. Because he was blind, his sense of hearing was very sharp indeed, and the music had sounded to him like nothing he had ever heard before. It seemed to be calling to him in a funny sort of way, and it sounded like a song that his mother had sung to him when he was a very little mole indeed, a long time ago.

He popped his head out from under the slate and peered about, unseeing.

"What's going on?" he called out.

The mice were many of them nearly back in the cottage, and the bats had started crawling back under the eaves.

"It's a truce!" said Jimmy Wheatear.

"And we're going back inside to have a jolly dance!"

"It's beautiful!" said the mole. And he began to perform a little dance himself. He raised his paws above his head and gave a little twirl. Then he stumbled over his own feet and fell over.

"I'm not used to doing this," he said apologetically.

"Come on, come on," said Samuel Crackling to the other mice. "Don't stand there all day watching him. Let him dance all night if he wants to."

But the mole wasn't going to be able to dance all night. At that moment a white shadow flew above him out of the dusk. It was the great O, who had himself been woken by the strange music and been extremely irritated by it. He had flown down from Skull Wood to see what it was, and here was this idiot mole dancing on a piece of slate.

It was like an offering on a plate! A ready-made meal!

So the great O swooped down and picked up the mole in his beak.

Oh, no!

Just when it had seemed that everything was going to end happily, the worst had happened. The real enemy had appeared.

The mice and the bats, though terrified, were prompted into action. Samuel Crackling raised his paw and ordered the matches to be struck and fired. Mr McFruit gave the signal for the bats to swoop with their curtain-hooks and needles.

O looked at them and was utterly astonished. These ridiculous creatures were not only singing and dancing and behaving like children, but they were hurling things at him. One lit match flipped through the air like a little caber, turning and turning, and hit his tail feathers, where it fizzled briefly without doing any harm.

The great god O was not only astonished, but amused. In fact he had to laugh.

"You little pygmies!" he called out scornfully.

"You insignificant shower of nothingness! You…
bits and pieces!"

Of course, in order to speak he had to open his
beak. The poor mole fell back on to the slate,
where the great O pinned him to it with one claw,
like keeping his place in a book he was reading. He
would get back to the mole when he had finished
rebuking these upstart mice and bats.

What could they do? Samuel Crackling's digger
raised its toy arms up and down, but he himself
was crouching behind it. Lit candle-stumps
flickered from the gutter and went out. The bats
peered from the eaves in terror. It was useless.

But one bat summoned up a little bit more
courage than the others. Just one bat out of all of
them. It was Bad Boy, with a needle in his teeth.
They had already managed to get the great O's
attention. He was still there, perched on the slate
with his claw on poor mole's back leg, preaching

at them in his hideous lordly way. Why not strike now?

Bad Boy fluttered up high above the chimney and then plunged. Down and down he went, faster and faster, towards the great O.

He was in luck. The needle stuck in O's head, and he was forced to let go of the mole.

Hooting with the stinging pain, O twisted his head round and round, trying to dislodge the needle with his wings. But the point had gone in right at the top of the head, and he just couldn't get to it. It was stuck in the centre of its target, like the stalk of an apple, his wings scraping at it ineffectively. O's dance was a sinister dance of his own, not a dance of joy but a mad dance of pain, the dance of a god who had been defied.

Everyone cheered, and Bad Boy made his way breathlessly back to the eaves.

The dazed mole was just able to limp his way

back into his tunnel, and quickly the mice and the bats re-entered the cottage, where they put away their weapons in safe places. Well! These weapons had nearly led them into a useless war, and most of them were pretty useless in themselves. But who would have thought that they could defy the great O like that? That would give him something to think about.

Red thought that perhaps he was somebody now, and that stories might in the future be told about him. But it was Bad Boy who was certainly the hero of the hour. Both of them were cheered and cheered. And the mice and bats danced together until midnight. They weren't going to listen any more to either Samuel Crackling or Mr McFruit.

At the close of the dancing, the mice sang together their song of fear to celebrate the peace, and the deliverance of the mole, and Red sang it as loudly as any of them:

> *Fear is what you thought you heard:*
> *Pad of beast and wing of bird.*
> *Fear is frozen in your track,*
> *Lonely when the night is black.*
> *Fear has left your breath behind.*
> *Heart is thudding in your mind.*
> *O and K, and K and O!*
> *There is one thing that they know!*

This was the thing that O and K knew, and O knew it in the fullness of his hot brain as he soared back above the stirring tops of the fir trees with the irritating needle stuck in his head: mice and bats and moles only existed to be eaten by the powerful creatures that lived in order to eat them. They were destined so to die, and Death was the greatest god of all.

O would never die. He was too powerful. His friend the raven would pull out the needle for him and he would live to find the mice another day.

Shadow saw him passing overhead, and thought he looked beautiful, but then knew that she shouldn't think such confusing thoughts if she could help it, for how could something so cruel be beautiful? That was the greatest mystery of all.

As O's own shadow passed over the moonlit fields, Gustave, the Duc d'Elbeuf, looked out from the window of his cosy parlour and saw it reflected upon the stream, and thought he should perhaps bolt his door. He, too, knew about fear.

And Simon Snee, the old snail, ever ready to shrink back into his inedible house, made his slow and slippery evening journey across the lawn. He did not think he had much to fear from the terrible O, but he was tired now, and like all the creatures of the hillside needed to get safely home. As he made his way, he sang more of his song, which like all songs said something of what he dimly knew about life and death:

When every drop of light is gone,
I'll rest from all my labours
And hang out with my neighbours
Beneath a stone.

And always I'll be quietly listening
For the first drops of rain,
When I will walk again,
Grey and glistening.

Day after day the dust will creep
And ashes clog the hearth.
Leaves scrape upon the path.
Better sleep.